"Let's begin, then," Ulrich said. "I want to get this over with."

Gaia's life, he meant. He wanted to get her life over with. He leaned down to her with the IV needle in his hand, and he began to tap her arm for the vein.

Jesus Christ. This was how she was going to die. Euthanized like a death row criminal. She almost wished she hadn't woken up. Because there was absolutely nothing she could do. No amount of fighting spirit could change anything. Her body was strapped so tightly to that bed, she could hardly move a muscle. Even if she could, she was too weak to make a dent in those leather straps.

Ulrich inserted the needle into her arm, and then he moved around to the other side of the bed to insert the second. Gaia searched her brain desperately for some answer, some brilliant scheme, but there was nothing. Literally no room to maneuver.

He inserted the needle into her other arm, and then he moved back around the bed to press the switch and end her life. *Maybe there is an afterlife,* she told herself. *And I've just been too cynical to believe it.*

Or maybe she just needed to believe that, in this last moment. Maybe she needed to believe a lot of things that she had never believed before.

Don't miss any books in this thrilling series:

FEARLESS™

Available from SIMON PULSE

FEARLESS™

GONE

FRANCINE PASCAL

SIMON PULSE
New York   London   Toronto   Sydney

First Simon Pulse edition November 2004

Copyright © 2004 by Francine Pascal

Cover copyright © 2004 by Alloy Entertainment

SIMON PULSE
An imprint of Simon & Schuster Children's Publishing Division
1230 Avenue of the Americas, New York, NY 10020

 Produced by Alloy Entertainment
151 West 26th Street
New York, NY 10001

All rights reserved, including the right of reproduction
in whole or in part in any form.
For information address Alloy Entertainment,
151 West 26th Street, New York, NY 10001.

Fearless™ is a trademark of Francine Pascal.

Printed in the United States of America
10 9 8 7 6 5 4 3 2 1

Library of Congress Control Number: 2004100274
ISBN: 0-689-86919-3

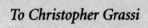
To Christopher Grassi

Dear Readers:

At last Gaia is graduating. Moving on to the rest of her life. But, in true Gaia style, it won't be ordinary. That's what has been so thrilling about Gaia for the last six years.

About ten years ago I read a small article in the *New York Times* about a woman who didn't seem to have any reaction to fear. I was fascinated. They couldn't give any scientific reason so I invented my own: obviously she was born without the fear gene. I loved the idea, now all I needed was the right girl. And I found her in Gaia. Gaia is just enough of a rebel and just enough of a hero to be the dream of every teenage girl. And she's not afraid of anything or anyone. What freedom!

It was easy to hit the right notes. All I had to do was pretend I was Gaia and everything worked. And I think that's what the readers did, too. You were able to lose yourselves in the fantasy of being Gaia Moore. Well, now, faithful fans and dreamers, I promise I won't let you down.

Though we are going to lose sight of Gaia for a while, she will turn up where we least expect. And with someone who will be a complete surprise. I can't tell you any more at this time. But, I promise, she will be back. You have been marvelous fans and I thank you so much for your loyalty.

Sincerely,

Francine Pascal

There were a
hundred

renegade

different

psycho

ways to

shut Jake

up.

GAIA MOORE HAD NEARLY FORGOTTEN
everything that made her
remarkable. It had been a nasty
state of affairs. Embarrassing.
Shameful, even. She'd found
herself drowning in the most
pathetic swamp of insecurity
and mediocrity and what she

The Great Confuser

could only term "generalized feminine namby-
pambyness." Over the last few weeks she seemed to
have completely forgotten that her IQ was genius
level, that her senses were superior to the average
human's, that she was trained in more martial arts
than she could count. In other words, that she had
more power in her little finger than Skyler Rodke and
his entire family combined.

But she was remembering now. Bit by bit. Piece by
piece. She was turning up her power in careful,
measured increments. And as she sprinted up
Morningside Drive, pumping her legs with forceful
ease to make it back to Skyler's apartment before he
did, she began to devise her plan of attack.

It would not be an "attack" in the usual sense of the
word. Skyler deserved a hell of a lot worse than just a
perfectly placed kick to the larynx or a punch to the
solar plexus. Given the apparent scope of the Rodkes'
plans, this attack was going to have to be strategic in
nature. She had to know every aspect of their plan;

then she could formulate the ideal response—the perfect counterpunch. She needed all her power now. She needed to be cool and composed and rational. And finally, without gobs of fear clouding her judgment, she could be all those things and more. Because she was free at last. Free of all that fear.

There was at least one thing she had learned during her temporarily frightened existence: fear was "the Great Confuser." All her bouts with terror had turned her brain into cafeteria oatmeal—weak and mushy and flavorless. That was Gaia in the presence of Skyler Rodke: weak and mushy. No *identity.* Which was just what he'd wanted. It's what they'd all wanted, apparently—Skyler and his father and Dr. Ulrich, too, which was pissing her off to no end. But that was all over now. Now she was paying attention. Now her thoughts were exquisitely pristine.

As she whipped around the corner of 121st Street, she replayed the entire scene she had just witnessed, or rather *heard,* in that generic medical facility on Bowery and Bleecker. She could still feel the aches in her joints from cramming herself inside that filing cabinet, but it had been worth it. She'd managed to eavesdrop on the Rodkes' "top secret" little meeting, and she'd heard at least some of what she'd needed to hear. She'd heard the voices of Skyler, his father, and Dr. Ulrich conspiring against her. And she'd heard that one new mystery man, although he wasn't such a mystery anymore, given the words Skyler had spoken in his presence: *army* and *soldiers*. Whoever the mystery man was, he was unquestionably military. Whatever the Rodkes were planning, the army was somehow involved.

But conspiracies were all in the details. And the details were precisely what she didn't have. They'd called off their little meeting too quickly, leaving Gaia with too little information and no choice but to wait it out inside that cabinet and then sneak out the back stairs of the building, making a break for it.

At least now she could begin to put all the pieces together. With each long stride down the street, she revved up that once-dormant part of her brain that could think with machinelike precision.

Think it through, she ordered herself. *What are the things you know? What are the things you don't know?* Her mind instantly split those two categories down the middle and formulated a simple informational chart:

Things I know:
1. *Skyler, Dr. Rodke, and Dr. Ulrich are the enemy.*
2. *They are concocting some kind of drug using my genes—using me as their own personal lab rat. That's at least one of the reasons they've been trying to keep me under lock and key and under Skyler's disgustingly chauvinistic influence.*
3. *The military is somehow involved.*

Things I don't know:

1. Just how extensive a family affair is this? Are Chris and Liz involved, too? Has our friendship just been part of the scam?

2. How *exactly* is the army involved? Does this go all the way up to top government levels, or are we just dealing with one renegade psycho general?

3. What the hell are they planning next?

4. The most important question of all: Whatever they're planning next. . . how am I going to stop *it*?

That was really all she cared about now as the sweat trickled down her temples and she took the steps of Skyler's building in leaps and bounds. She just needed to figure out how to stop them all. By herself—that was an absolute. That was not up for debate. She was putting an end to this entire mystery operation alone.

At the very least she knew what *she* had to do next. . . as sick as it was going to make her. She had to maintain the status quo. She had to continue to play the part of the `frightened, mushy-headed girlie-girl` with Skyler. She had to continue to play scared and "kept" in his presence, until she could gather all the necessary info without him even knowing it. Because right now, all she had going for her was the element of surprise. Her most valuable weapon wasn't the power she had finally rediscovered; it was that Skyler didn't *know* she had rediscovered it. And Gaia was going to keep it that way. Until just the perfect moment. Then she would let him know. Then she'd remind them all just exactly who they were dealing with.

JAKE COULDN'T KEEP ALL HIS THOUGHTS in line. That was something he'd have to work on if he truly planned to make it in the world of covert ops. He'd have to learn how to organize all the facts in his head and draw clear-

Ultraviolent Medicine

cut conclusions. Then he'd have to learn how to keep those conclusions separate from the mishmash of emotions twirling around in his head like paint in an industrial mixer. Because right now he sucked at it. He couldn't help it. His heart was mangled with frustration.

He had seen the truth. He'd seen the infamous "God" dealing Invince in Washington Square Park, and now he knew that "God" was in fact none other than Chris Rodke himself, disguised in cheap spray-on blue hair dye and blue wraparound shades and a long

Matrix-style coat. Now he knew that Chris had been the one dealing Invince to the entire city, wrecking New Yorkers' lives (including Gaia's, Ed's, Kai's, and even his own) with "a bit of the old ultraviolence." That in and of itself made Jake sick to his stomach. It made him want to find "God," aka Chris, and give him a whopping dose of his own ultraviolent medicine.

But the situation ran much deeper than just one drug dealer, and Jake knew it—even if he didn't understand exactly how. Chris might be the distributor, but Jake was pretty sure that the true source of Invince was Rodke and Simon itself. And Jake was convinced that the entire operation had something to do with Gaia. . . *something*—that was all he knew. But still, he could *feel* it: Gaia was the Rodkes' victim. She was their target. And this was where Jake's emotions were getting the better of him. This was truly pissing him off.

Because Gaia was too goddamn blind to *see* it.

How could she let herself get snowed by that faux "playah" rich boy Skyler Rodke and his snob of a brother? And more importantly, why couldn't she see that she needed more capable people to step in and take care of things for her? Jake and Oliver were the ones who really knew what was going on here. Not only did they know what was going on, they were the ones who could *handle* it. Why couldn't Gaia see that?

Jake whipped his cell phone out of his pocket and

dialed Gaia's cell number. He could just picture her right now, leaning her misguided head on Skyler's shoulder, staring up at that asshole's face with a trusting smile, being snowed by every single lie coming out of his puckered-up little blue-blood mouth. For all Jake knew, Gaia was sitting there with Skyler *and* Chris, having a freaking wine tasting or something. It was time to give Gaia a serious reality check.

He listened through her voice mail message (of course she still refused to pick up her phone), and the moment he heard that beep, he just let it rip.

"Gaia, I thought we *talked* about this," he barked into the phone. "You've got to *pick up* when I call." He took a deep breath and tried to clamp down on his frustration before placing the phone back to his ear. "All right, listen, okay. *Listen* to me this time, 'cause I'm not screwing around here. Chris Rodke is 'God,' do you understand? *Chris* is the one dealing Invince in the park. I was *there*, all right? I saw it with my own eyes. If you want to know why we nearly got killed in the park by those psychos—if you wanna know why Ed and Kai were almost *killed*, it's because of your friend Chris. And this goes deep, Gaia, Oliver and I are sure of it. This whole operation stems back to the whole Rodke family. As in Mr. "Upstanding CEO." As in Mr. Upstanding CEO's son *Skyler*. Do you get it now? They're plotting something against you, Gaia.

We're sure of it. They're using you. If you're still sitting there in Skyler's house, then you need to *get out*. You need to get out of that apartment right now and you need to contact me and Oliver. You need to let us take care of this thing. And if you can't get out of that apartment, then you need to let us know *where* it is. Give us Skyler's location and we'll come there and get you out. Just *call us*. I'll be at Oliver's in ten minutes, and we'll wait for your call. Look, I know I sound pissed, but I'm just worried. I'm worried you're not seeing the whole picture here. So just call, okay? And stay away from Skyler Rodke. And Gaia, whatever you do, stay the hell away from Chris. He's sick in the head. The whole family is."

Poster Child

EVERYONE IN THE ENTIRE RODKE building knew Chris. Every secretary, every janitor, and more importantly, every security guard. It was part of their job—knowing when the boss's son was rolling through, knowing which butt to kiss to get their Christmas bonus. Chris sped through a chorus of obsequious hellos as he made his way through the gilded revolving doors of Rodke Industries, straight

9

through the metal detectors, and into the elevator, banging on the button six or seven times, as if that would somehow speed things along. He had absolutely no time to waste. He was doing damage control here, and that meant moving swiftly and keeping his mounting anxiety to a minimum. Which wasn't so easy at this particular moment. Because the proverbial cat was out of the bag.

Jake had seen him in the park and Chris knew it. God's identity had been revealed. Chris was sure that Jake was sitting somewhere right now feeling quite proud of his successful little spy job, but that didn't matter to Chris in the least. Dealing with Jake would be easy. He surely had no idea what God was capable of. There were a hundred different ways to shut Jake up. The problem was his father. Chris had to be the one to tell his father about this unfortunate development before he heard it from anyone else. And when his father heard the news... he wouldn't be happy.

And screw him for being such a pompous, neglectful son of a bitch, Chris thought as he tapped his foot incessantly and waited for each floor to race by. *This is my father's fault anyway. If he'd given me just an ounce of additional support—a couple of lookouts, a little protection—this never would have happened. And isn't Skyler just going to love this?* Chris gnashed his teeth together as the elevator opened on the executive floor. This was just what Skyler needed to prove that Chris was nothing but a screwup. Wouldn't this just support every little snide comment and obnoxious insult his brother and father had not so subtly thrown at him? *"You're not careful, Chris." "Your tasteless flare for drama just embarrasses us." "One more of your stupid stunts and you'll ruin the Rodke name permanently."*

That phrase had always stuck in Chris's head like black tar: *"Tasteless flare for drama. . ."* He knew exactly what it implied, no matter how much his father and brother denied it—no matter how many times Chris had denied it himself. It was a veiled code for "gay." Of course, his family had always insisted to the hilt that they had no problem with his sexuality. They'd made Chris a poster child for "acceptance" in all the society magazines and press releases, and Chris had always tried to believe the party line. He'd convinced himself that his own flesh and blood were too enlightened and intelligent to be prejudiced. And as far as his mother and Liz were concerned, he still believed it. But if he was being completely honest with himself, then he had to face his serious doubts about his father and Skyler. They could *appear* as enlightened as they wanted, but there was at least one category where Chris knew his sexuality was an issue: the Family Business. He'd tried to deny it a hundred times before, but it was getting harder and harder to turn a blind eye. Never in a million years would they have come out and said it, but now Chris could feel them thinking it: "We don't want the gay boy running the company."

The fact was, his mother and Liz were the only ones in this family who'd shown Chris the realest kind of affection and respect. They were the only ones who'd treated him with love and kindness even when they *didn't* have guests over or the paparazzi flashing away at some horrific promotional event. That's when his father's arm was suddenly draped all over Chris's shoulders and he had a wide, loving grin. That's when his father would fake-smile his way through some inane conversation with Chris until the camera crew had shut off their lights and gone home. It was sickening.

By the time Chris had made it to his father's office, the anxiety had already given way to anger. Chris wasn't scared about admitting his screwup anymore. He wasn't scared of anything or anyone. Especially his father. He wasn't scared. What was there to be scared of? This wasn't his fault. It was not his fault.

So why was he sweating so profusely?

Chris stiffened his posture and swallowed very hard. Then he stared down at his father's secretary, Eileen, with a cold "I-own-you" glare. There was no time for his usual fake princely smile.

"I need to speak with my dad, Eileen," Chris stated. "Now."

Eileen's insecurity began to bleed out through her caked-on makeup and her excessive eye shadow—the low-class giveaways to her buttoned-up "executive assistant" facade.

"You'll have to wait, Chris," she said, trying to sound firm and professional. "Your father just came in with an important client, and he said no visitors."

"*Visitors?*" Chris squawked. "Do I strike you as a *visitor*, Eileen?"

"No, of course not," Eileen croaked. "I'm just telling you. . . he insisted they not be disturbed. . . ."

"Disturbed? Do you think he would find a visit from his own son disturbing?"

Eileen's eyes widened nervously. "No, Chris, no, I just—"

"Right, I'll only be a minute."

"Chris. . ."

Eileen stood out of her chair, but Chris ignored her completely, marching right by and swinging open the double doors to his father's office.

Two angry faces darted up toward the doorway. Chris had seen this look on his father's face a thousand times. But the other man he had never seen before. And given his crisp, tightly buttoned army uniform and the regalia of stars and bars on his shoulders, Chris certainly would have remembered him.

Dr. Rodke quickly wiped the dark frown from his face and replaced it with the fakest smile of delight. "Chris!" he bellowed jovially. "What a surprise! Listen, we're right in the middle of something here—why don't you give us just a few minutes and then you and I can go to lunch?"

Chris's eyes darted down to his father's grand mahogany desk. There were numerous copies of some kind of contract spread out across the desk, and General Stars and Bars had clearly been right in the middle of signing one of them. Not only did this make Chris extremely curious, but if there was one thing he couldn't tolerate, it was being dismissed by his father. He took a large step into the room and matched his father's disgusting display of fakery with a display of his own.

"Ooh, Daddy, can I just get a few minutes with you now?" He clasped his hands together in prayer and bounced slightly in place. "I've got a problem I really need your help with. *Pleeease*. I'm drowning in teenage angst!" Chris knew exactly what he was doing. He was challenging his father's supposed tolerance right to his face. He was "turning up the gay." And it was making his father squirm. Chris turned to General Stars and Bars and waived daintily. "Hiii. I'm Chris."

The general raised his right eyebrow with contempt, although the rest of his craggy, tight-lipped face didn't budge. Dr. Rodke bolted up from his chair with another plastered-on smile. "Um. . . General Colter, this is my son Christopher. Chris. . . General Colter."

So Stars and Bars had a name. That still didn't

explain what he was doing signing contracts in his father's office or why his father looked so uncomfortable. This meeting was clearly something Chris wasn't supposed to see. Which meant that he needed to see much, much more.

General Colter stood up slowly and shook Chris's hand. "Good to meet you." His handshake nearly broke Chris's fingers.

"You too," Chris said. "Listen, General, could you please just give me and my dad a minute? See, I'm having 'boy problems.' I *love* your outfit, by the way." Chris smiled.

General Colter looked mortified, and Chris savored every moment of it. The general stared at Chris and then flashed his father a dubious glance. "Why don't I give you two a minute," he said finally.

"Oh, God *bless* you." Chris grinned. "It'll only be a sec!" Chris held the door open for the general and then slammed it closed behind him. The smile instantly dropped from his face.

Chris's father glared at him with even deeper disdain than usual. "What the hell are you doing?" He clenched his teeth to keep his volume in check. "If you're trying to embarrass me, then congratulations—"

"What am *I* doing?" Chris snapped. "What are *you* doing? What kind of deal are we making with him? What, did the army run out of no-tears shampoo or something?"

15

"Chris, keep your voice down. This is not the time or place for this. Go back to school. Go back to school, and I'll see you at dinner."

"Not until you tell me what's going on here." Chris stepped over to the desk and picked up one of the contracts, but his father swiped it from his hand.

"Chris, this has nothing to do with you, all right? This is none of your concern."

"Oh, the family business is none of my concern now?"

"*This* is none of your concern. Go back to school, or go home, or go anywhere. Just go. We will talk *later*."

"No, I'd rather stay, thanks." Chris plopped down in his father's chair and threw his feet up on the desk. "Let's bring General Colter back in—maybe he'll tell me what's going on." Chris reached for the phone, but his father slammed it back down.

"Enough!" Dr. Rodke hissed. There was so much anger in his father's eyes, Chris actually caught himself flinching, but he covered it immediately. And somewhere in that moment, Chris finally realized what an idiot he was being.

This was about the drug. Of course. This was about their entire operation. They were making some kind of deal with the military, and Chris wasn't supposed to know a thing about it. They were keeping him completely out of the loop. "The army?" Chris uttered. "We're working with the army?" Blood rushed to his face with each word. His nails dug into his palms. "When exactly were you going to tell me? When was anyone going to tell me what we were planning here?"

"*We* are not planning anything, Chris. *Skyler* and I are planning. You did your part. You did your job, and now it's done. So you can go now, and you can spend some of my money, or throw yourself one of your parties, or whatever it is you do, and your brother and I will take it from here. Do you understand?"

Each word was more condescending than the last. Chris could feel the humiliation gathering in his chest like an infection. He looked his father deep in the eye. "*I* am your son, too, asshole. And in case you haven't noticed, I have practically been running this entire thing myself, risking my life out there in the scummiest parts of this city for you, while your favorite son has been 'handling' the oh-so-challenging task of flirting with jailbait. So why won't you give me some freaking *respect*, goddammit?"

"Shut up!" His father dug his fingers into Chris's arm and tugged him brutally out of his chair. "I told you to keep your voice down. Christ, I've tried to be patient with you, but I am so sick of your whining. You want my respect, Chris? You want my respect? Then stop acting like a *child*. Look at you. You come prancing in here like a spoiled schoolboy who wants his daddy. Like some goddamn drama queen starring in

17

the school play. What do you think that man out there thinks of me now? You made me look like a *fool*, Chris. And if you blow this deal for us, I swear to God. . . Look, I just want you out of here. Now. I want you miles away from this office, from this deal, from *any* deal this company is trying to make. Here's how to earn my respect, Chris: Stop embarrassing the hell out of me. And if you really must hear me say it, then I'll say it. Learn how to be more like your brother."

"Like my—?"

"Like a *man*, Chris. Stop prancing around and *be* a *man*."

Ugly silence filled the room.

It was by far the closest his father had ever come to actually saying it: *If you want my respect, then stop being gay.* Chris was so furious, he could barely breathe.

"You want to see a child?" Chris uttered. "You want to see what a child acts like? This is what a child acts like."

Chris slammed his hands down on the desk, scrunched the contracts in his hands, and threw them up into the air with every ounce of pubescent tantrum he had in him.

"Goddammit!" his father hollered, crouching to the floor to collect the mess. "Get out!"

But the truth was, this was no tantrum. Chris's rage had already moved way past tantrum into that beautifully calm zone of anger, where everything became very cold and very distant and very calculated. The tantrum was in fact a distraction. The moment his father crouched to the floor, Chris grabbed one of the contracts and stuffed it inside his bag.

His reason for stealing the copy of the contract was simple. If he was going to exact revenge on his father and Skyler, he would need to know everything they'd been planning.

Because that's what a *man* would do, right? When a man is shunned by his own family, a man seeks revenge.

Apparently
all of New
York City
was just **brazen**
a cage
full of lab **joy**
rats to the
Rodke
brothers.

IT WAS ONLY AN HOUR BUS RIDE

Big, Beautiful Blur

out to Carverton, New York, and Ed was glad he'd done it. He certainly didn't mind taking the rest of the day off from school, and it had given his ears a break from the incessant prom chatter of the FOHs. His last few second-semester-senior classes hardly counted as classes anyway.

The odd thing was, the moment he creaked open Heather's door at Carverton School for the Blind, a huge grin came over Heather's beautiful face. Did Heather just smile whenever anyone walked into her room now?

The first words out of her mouth confused him even further. "Edward H. Fargo." She smiled. "You freaking stud."

Ed's eyes widened as a tentative smile cropped up on his own face. "Wait. . . How did you know it was me?"

"It's that raggedy-ass yellow T-shirt." She laughed. "It just screams 'Ed.'"

Ed peered deeper into Heather's eyes as her smile began to grow. "No way. . ." A rush of excitement ran up his spine. "You can see me?"

Heather stood up from her desk and walked slowly toward him. She reached out her hands and placed them on either side of his face. "I can see you," she whispered.

Her eyes welled up slightly, and then she threw her arms around him, giving him a huge bear hug.

It truly was like going back in time.

The hug went on and on until Heather finally pulled away and looked into Ed's eyes. "I mean. . . I can *sort of* see you," she explained. "You are a complete blur, but you are stunningly gorgeous. Come! Sit down." She grabbed his hand and dragged him over to her bed, where they both plopped down, face-to-face.

Ed hardly knew where to start, given this incredible development. He couldn't form much of a sentence. "I don't. . . I mean, that's just. . . What happened?"

"It just *started*," Heather announced, throwing her arms up in the air. She was absolutely beaming. "I just woke up one morning two weeks ago and there were these spots. And then a few days later there were some colors, and then it all just sort of *opened up*. . . into this big, beautiful blur. I mean, the doctors had always said there was a good chance I'd recover, and some days I didn't believe them, but then I would think about *you*, Ed. The way you dealt with everything and the way you worked and worked when you knew there might be a chance to walk. That's why I wanted you to be the first person to come. I wanted you to be the first person from back home who I can *see*. I mean, besides my parents. And you, Mr. Fargo, are such a sight for sore eyes." She laughed, gazing at Ed for another moment, and then she burst forward and threw her arms around him again. Ed was forced to swipe a tiny and extremely embarrassing tear from the corner of his eye. He hoped it was all too much of a blur for Heather to notice.

Ed was so genuinely elated for Heather that her joke didn't even seem corny. Although he still felt it would be too corny to tell her that he'd felt the exact same way the moment he'd walked through the door. Heather truly was a sight for sore eyes. This was exactly what he'd needed. A blast from the past. Something *real*. A very real bit of good news from a very old friend. This was something to celebrate. A beginning, not an ending. No glitzy gown or tuxedo required.

Ed studied Heather's face, from her silken brown hair to her red-flushed cheeks to her perfect little chin. "I'm just. . . I'm really happy for you."

"But wait." She grinned. "There's *more*."

"What? What else could there possibly be?"

"Well. . . I asked you to come for another reason, Ed."

"Oh, really?" He cracked a dubious half smile. "And what is that?"

"Well, here's the thing." She giggled. "What with the considerable lack of a social life here at Carverton, I have been working my *ass* off making up all my missing credits. And after much red tape, and many phone calls between principals, and a *considerable* amount of charm on my part. . . they're going to let me graduate with you guys!"

"Aha." Ed smiled. "Sweet. That's awesome, Heather."

Heather took a series of small bows. "Thank you, thank you. Yet. . . there is *still* more."

"Yikes."

"Not only can I graduate with the class, but after inflicting another dose of considerable charm on my parents. . . I can go to the prom! As long as I have a chaperone that they 'know and trust.'"

Quite suddenly Heather dropped her head and stared down at the bedsheets. Her brazen joy had all but disappeared, replaced by a most uncharacteristic attack of what looked an awful lot like. . . shyness? "I was going to call you. . . ," she uttered quietly, "but now that you're here. . . I was, you know. . . kind of hoping. . ." Her eyes drifted along the entire bed over to the floor. "Well, kind of *praying*, actually. . . that *you* would take me." She finally turned back up to Ed, squinting tentatively, as if to shield herself from a potential blow. "Would you, Ed. . . ? Would you take me to the prom?"

Ed went silent. He felt the most bittersweet pain in his chest. This he had not expected. Not just her request, but the way she had asked it. With such sweetness and insecurity—and *sweet* and *insecure* were two adjectives that no one ever would have used to describe Heather Gannis back in the day.

He thought he had come here to reminisce—to

24

relive the old days. But this moment had only served to remind him just how much things had changed. Somewhere along the way, Heather Gannis had become humble. Just a year or two ago, if Heather Gannis had approached Ed Fargo and asked *him* to the prom? It would have been like some kind of dream sequence—Shred the skater boy's secret little fantasy. But now a year ago felt like a thousand years. And as much as Ed had been hoping to go back in time, this was his wake-up call. That was then, and this was now.

Heather looked so vulnerable, he could hardly get the words out. The last thing he wanted to do was poke holes in her hard-earned happiness. But he really had no choice. Now he found himself squinting, too, just to get the words out.

"I . . . I can't," he said.

Heather's shoulders slumped slightly forward, and her head began to drop again, but she quickly raised it and forged some version of a smile on her lips.

"I'm sorry," Ed added quickly.

"That's okay."

"I really am."

"It's *okay*," she assured him with a forced chuckle. "I know it's a little late in the game to be asking."

"Yeah, I just . . . I already have a date."

Heather couldn't help but raise a curious eyebrow. Her eyes even brightened a bit. *"Gaia?"*

"Oh, *nooo*," Ed assured her, waving his hands as if the suggestion were insane. "Jesus, why would you even ask that? We barely speak."

"I know. But for a second there I thought she might have come to her senses in the end."

Ed's entire face contorted with disbelief. "What are you talking about?"

Heather crossed her arms and gave Ed a long stare. "Ed, come on. The girl's in love with you. She always has been."

Ed coughed out a tragic laugh. "You really have been gone a long time."

"Oh, *please*, Ed. Love is love."

"Yeah, right. . ." Once again Heather had managed to induce a bittersweet pain in Ed's chest. Not to mention twist his stomach into knots. He had to change the subject. "Well, anyway, I am most definitely not going with Gaia. I'm going with this girl Kai from school. It's a totally platonic deal," he added, although he wasn't sure why. "I mean. . . you know. . . she's cool. We sort of started a thing, but. . . it wasn't really that kind of a thing. She's a good friend. I mean. . . pretty good."

"Well, that's nice," Heather said, looking unconvinced. "So then who is Gaia going with?"

Ed cringed. It was his least favorite topic. "I don't really know. Jake Montone maybe or this Skyler guy. Haven't Megan and Melanie been keeping you constantly informed?"

Heather snorted. "Yeah, sure, they've sent me a lot of babble-gossip e-mails about it, but who would be dumb enough to believe them? God, after all this time they're still so obsessed with Gaia. It's tragic."

"I know."

"Low self-esteem."

"Yeah. . ."

Now they both went silent. Somewhere along the way, this jubilant little reunion had taken a wrong turn. Heather finally let out a small sigh as she stared back at the floor.

"I'm really sorry I can't go with you," Ed said, trying to catch her eyes. "I totally would if I hadn't already—"

"No, it's not that," Heather interrupted. "It's not that."

"Oh." He searched Heather's eyes. "Then what?"

She let out a much longer sigh this time, turning to gaze out the small window of her room. "I don't know. It's just. . . we've been through *so much crap,* Ed. All this violence, and all this tragedy, and all this pain. And we made it. I mean, we're alive. You can walk. I can *see.* There should be some sort of celebration, you know? A huge one. Maybe that's what the prom is for, I don't know. And maybe it will be, but. . . look at us." She turned back to him, raising her eyebrows. "I mean, don't get me wrong: I am so grateful for what I have. I have my sight back. I get to graduate with you guys. I have *you* here. But God. . . our lives are so different. We're so different. I'm not even saying that's a bad thing, it's just. . . I can't speak for you, but this is definitely *not* where I thought I'd be when graduation came around."

"I know," Ed said. Boy, did he know. He knew all too well.

GAIA FELT TWO QUICK VIBRATIONS

Appropriately Oblivious

against her hip as she slammed the door to Skyler's apartment. Some-one had left her a voice mail.

She quickly parked herself on the couch with a magazine, making sure she would look appropriately oblivious for Skyler's entrance. She'd made it back in time. He'd have no idea she'd ever left—no idea she'd witnessed his entire secret meeting. She wiped the sweat from her face with her sleeve and reshuffled her hair into a smooth ponytail. Then she took a moment to subdue her breathing after her marathon sprint from the subway station. Once she was calm and collected, she ripped her cell from her pocket and checked the message.

"You have. . . one. . . new message," the cold-hearted phone lady announced. And then came Jake's booming voice. His voice was so loud and intense, she had to pull the phone back from her ear just to listen.

"Gaia, I thought we *talked* about this. . . ," he growled.

"Ugh, Jake, calm down," she muttered, as if Jake could somehow hear her. But then she heard Jake's voice utter these words:

"Chris Rodke is 'God,' do you understand? Chris is the one dealing Invince in the park. . . ."

Her body froze. The truth was suddenly echoing thought her head, buzzing like an insect lodged inside her ear—the despicable truth about Chris Rodke, her supposed *friend*. So Chris was a part of it, too. A *huge* part of it. Now she knew for sure. It was hardly even a surprise at this point. The Rodkes' little pharmaceutical plot just grew sicker by the minute. It seemed Gaia wasn't their only lab rat. Every skinhead and Invince freak in the park was a lab rat, too. Apparently all of New York City was just a cage full of lab rats to the Rodke brothers.

Her entire body was aching to rise up immediately and hunt Chris down so she could riddle his body with kicks and punches. She could picture herself doing it—laying into Chris's skinny frame with every ounce of her rage—one kick to the face for every act of violence those "Droogs" had done to her and to Jake and to the countless other innocent victims that she didn't even know. And then, finally, a body slam—one brutal, spine-cracking body slam—for what they'd done to Ed.

But she could do none of the above. Not right now. Because she could hear the key entering the lock of the front door. And right now she had to fold up all that rage and stash it away somewhere. Right now she had to give Skyler Rodke the performance of a lifetime.

Rule number one: Appear startled.

This was something she would have to watch very closely in Skyler's company. If she was going to keep him in the dark, she needed to act just as skittish and rattled as she had been before. She tried to remember all her old pathetic behaviors. Behaviors she would much rather have forgotten.

As Skyler shoved the door open, she threw her hand over her heart and let out her best approximation of a gasp. "Jesus, you *scared* me," she said, locking her eyes with his as he closed the door behind him. Her father had taught her a great deal about lying in a crisis situation. The golden rule of lying: Always maintain eye contact.

"Sorry." Skyler smiled, dropping his keys on the side table. "Didn't mean to scare you. Who are you talking to?" He tilted his head quizzically.

Now, with a clear head, she was easily noticing all the little giveaways that she had been missing before. Skyler was so obviously suspicious and uncomfortable whenever she had the least bit of contact with the outside world. The Rodkes wanted her all to themselves.

"It's a message," she replied. She knew she should have shoved her phone back in her pocket when she heard the door being unlocked, but in this case an exception had to be made. She had to be sure Jake wasn't going to drop any more bombshells on her voice mail.

"Jeez, who's leaving the message?" Skyler giggled, sitting himself down on the couch as close to Gaia and her phone as he could possibly get. "He sounds pissed. I can hear him shouting from here."

"It's Jake," Gaia said, rolling her eyes for effect.

Rule number two: Tell as few lies as possible.

Another key lesson Gaia had learned in her crisis training. The key to a good cover was to stick to truthful statements as often as possible. This way you didn't get overloaded with lies to remember and maintain.

"Well, what's his problem?" Skyler asked.

"What*ever*," she groaned, quickly punching the key on her phone to delete his message the second he was done. No more bombshells, thank God. She shoved the phone back in her pocket and turned to Skyler. "He's still freaking out about this whole stupid prom thing," she lied. "He's not thrilled that you're taking me. Hell hath no fury like a macho man scorned."

"God, what a loser." Skyler sighed. He smiled at Gaia, but she could still detect the slightest suspicion in his eyes. And her instincts told her what she needed to do next if she truly wanted to shake that suspicion. It was the one classic female spy tactic she had thankfully always managed to avoid. Perhaps because she knew that she would be very bad at it. But if there was ever a time to use it, she felt the time was now, no matter how much nausea it was going to induce.

The fact was, Gaia had always tried to avoid the sexual tension issue with Skyler—even when it was staring her right in the face. Even on that most unfortunate occasion when she had actually let him bathe her, she'd tried to desexualize it in her head, convincing herself that his intentions were noble. But God help her, she was about to change that. She was about to bring it right out into the open. Because she was forming a plan of her own.

Her skin was crawling already. . . .

Memo

From: L
To: KS4

Need all KS ops to report in now. Any sight-
ings of CR yet? What is the holdup?

Memo

From: KS4
To: L

Nothing yet. Have extended the search area,
but still no signs. Any further leads from J?

Memo

From: L
To: KS4

J will be reporting in, but this is *unsatisfactory*
work. Subject is still out of pocket and under the
influence. Have your team redouble its efforts and
get me some intelligence on CR location ASAP.

"WHAT TOOK YOU SO LONG?" OLIVER was glaring at Jake in the doorway.

"I got here as fast as I could," Jake said, slipping by him. He made a bee-line for the kitchen sink, poured himself a glass of water, and guzzled it down.

Ten Lashes

Oliver followed him to the kitchen, itching with impatience. "Well, have you spoken with her or not?" he demanded.

Jake lowered his head and then poured himself another glass. "I left her a message," he uttered almost inaudibly. "She still hasn't gotten back to me—"

"A *message*. We don't have time for *phone tag*, Jake."

"I know, all right? I know." Jake dodged Oliver's disappointed glare and moved to the couch, plopping down in a heap and running his hand through his hair. "If she won't pick up her phone, there's nothing I can do about it. . . . I'm sorry."

Oliver took a breath and calmed himself. He tried to dial down his own frustration and lighten his expression. Gaia's stubbornness was a force to be reckoned with, he knew that. This fiasco wasn't Jake's fault any more than it was his own. But still, his temper was getting more and more difficult to control.

"This is unacceptable," Oliver muttered. "Unacceptable."

He paced the length of his spacious loft. "I've got an entire surveillance crew out there looking for this Chris Rodke, or *God*, or whatever the hell he calls himself. They've checked the park, they've checked the Rodke residence, they've checked the school, and *nothing*." He turned to Jake. "Where the hell is this boy?! Why has he suddenly gone into hiding?"

"I don't *know*," Jake said defensively.

"Well, does he know you're on to him?"

Jake paused. "What?"

"Did he *see* you see him?"

Oliver could see a sudden thought flash through Jake's head. His silence was answer enough, and it was making Oliver's blood start to simmer again. "Jake..."

"No," Jake insisted. "I mean, I don't think he saw me.... I mean, maybe."

Oliver stomped his foot down on the floor, sending a tremor through every piece of glass in the room. "Maybe? What do you mean, maybe?"

"Look, calm down, all right? He might have seen me, I'm not sure. This chick Zan thinks he saw me, but she's this drugged-out head case and I don't think she knows what she's talking about. Besides, even if he did see me, that's not going to make some guy who calls himself 'God' go run and hide. He's way too much of an egomaniac for that. I mean, if he *is* hiding right now, he's got to have a bigger reason than me."

"And when exactly did you develop this expertise in criminal profiling?"

Jake had no answer for that.

Oliver's hands began to form fists. He crammed the fists into his pockets and stepped over to Jake, towering over him on the couch. "Listen to me, Jake. . . This idiotic, overprivileged boy is the key. He has everything we need. He's got the drug. He's got the evidence we need to expose his whole family. He knows everything they are planning. He can point us straight to Gaia. We need to *find* this boy if we want to find *her*. And if you have screwed this up. . . if *you* are the reason we've lost him, I swear to God—"

"All right, stop!" Jake stood up from the couch and faced Oliver head-on.

"Stop what?"

"Stop looking at me like that."

"I don't know what you're talking about."

"Look, I'm not your son, all right? So stop looking at me like I'm about to get ten lashes with your belt."

"Don't be ridiculous."

"Well, the look in your eyes is freaking me out. So knock it off."

Oliver locked his eyes with Jake's. His entire body became brittle and tense. He would not tolerate anyone talking back to him like that. Especially not some inexperienced teenage nobody. Ten lashes with a belt was nothing compared to what Oliver could do to him. . . .

But one deep breath later, Oliver recovered his senses. He took a step back. What was he doing? He didn't have time to waste on this kind of petty infighting. He needed Jake.

"I'm sorry," he conceded, barely opening his mouth to speak.

"It's okay," Jake assured him. "I know how you feel. I feel the exact same way. We both just want her back here safe and sound. We just need to hear from her, that's all." Jake stepped away from Oliver and checked his phone for messages, but there were none. "Come *on*, Gaia. Call us, goddammit."

Oliver stood in place, staring out the window at the lower edge of Manhattan. Jake was right. He wasn't Oliver's son. Oliver didn't have a son. But he had Gaia. And that little Rodke bastard was not going to keep them apart.

And here's
to the birth
of the
bravest **sexual**
soldiers **tension**
the world
has ever
seen.

Minions

CHRIS HAD CHECKED HIMSELF INTO the Soho Grand under another name, and he'd paid cash. He'd taken one of the smaller rooms at the back of the hotel rather than his usual choice of the penthouse suite with the windows facing outward. He was quite sure that his father had noticed the missing military contract by now, and he'd definitely have his people out there looking for Chris. It wouldn't be the first time Robert Rodke had sent out his minions to search for his son. He'd done it for lesser reasons: a couple of drunken runaway attempts, a few shameless disappearing acts. . . anything to get a little attention.

But this was far more serious. Obviously his dad couldn't have a copy of this contract floating around in the open, and finally, with some quiet and some privacy, Chris could get a good look and find out why. He reached into his bag, pulled out the crumpled-up contract, and smoothed it out on the black minimalist desk. It was about twenty pages long, but the cover letter told the entire story. . . .

RODKE PHARMACEUTICALS, INC.

CONFIDENTIAL DOC. # 4417
LEVEL-ONE EXECUTIVES ONLY (CODE 24C)

General John T. Colter
Base 9 Training Facility—Sub. D. 5
1485 Avenue Tombalbaye BP 9070
Kinshasa, DR Congo

RE: OPERATION LIONHEART
General Colter,

Attached is Copy 5 of the aforementioned contract between *Rodke Pharmaceuticals, Inc.,* and *Base 9 Training Facility, Republic of Congo.*

As discussed, I, Robert Rodke, of Rodke Pharmaceuticals, Inc., do hereby guarantee full confidentiality and nondisclosure regarding all aspects of OPERATION LIONHEART.

SUMMARY OF AMENDED TERMS
AS AGREED TO BY BOTH PARTIES:

1. Rodke Pharmaceuticals, Inc., will provide 40 units of the compound "Invince" to

General Colter's army trainees in Base 9, Republic of Congo (60 pills per unit).

2. The drug will be administered orally for a test period of 60 days under the strict supervision of Dr. Karl Ulrich.

3. The drug will be one hundred percent free of all side effects and will provide the soldiers with one hundred percent fear suppression for the duration of the test period.

4. Upon conclusion of a successful test period, Rodke Pharmaceuticals will then enter into a long-term military contract with Base 9, providing 400 units of "Invince" per annum—Bases 10 and 11 to follow (see part 35B for details of future and permanent arrangement).

5. These terms (and all attached) shall remain TOP SECRET and CONFIDENTIAL for a minimum duration of 100 years (see part 44E).

I assume you are comfortable with all of the above terms (and the terms herein) and are prepared to sign all copies of the contract.

Here's to the mutual success of this auspicious

endeavor. And here's to the birth of the bravest soldiers the world has ever seen. It has been a great pleasure doing business with you.

Signed,

Robert Rodke
Chairman, President & CEO
Rodke Pharmaceuticals, Inc.

So it's real. It's actually
real. I just couldn't believe it
until I saw it in print. This is
what they've been planning all
along without ever letting me in
on a stitch of it. Not one goddamn whisper about it in my presence. At least now I know for
sure what I've always suspected
for years:

My brother and my father are
freaking lunatics. I am the only
sane man in my family.

They're going to give Invince
to *soldiers?* Have they completely
lost their minds? "one hundred
percent free of all side effects"?
Are you *kidding* me, Dad? "The
bravest soldiers the world has
ever seen"? Try the *craziest.*
Haven't you been listening to anything I've been telling you?
Haven't you read the newspaper
lately? Have you by any chance
noticed what Invince does to people? Because I've seen it first-
hand. And it's not pretty.

This is not what I signed up

for. Not at all. I thought we were developing a pill for years down the line. We were trying to make the perfect *anti-anxietal* pill. We were going to blow Prozac and Xanax right out of the water.

Yes, I did some pretty despicable deeds, but sometimes despicable deeds are the only way to make good things happen. A lot of people have to die before you can figure out how to cure a disease. That's just the way it goes. And I thought we were working to cure the worst disease in the world: fear. That's why I chose the name "God"—because I was doing the greatest work of all. I was going to save all the frightened souls of the world. I mean, Jesus, wouldn't that qualify me as the goddamn Messiah?

But all I was really doing was helping my father and Skyler sell another weapon to the army. They weren't just keeping me in the dark: they were flat-out lying to me. About everything. The same way they're lying now to that idiot Colter.

They used me. The same way
they used Gaia, the same way
I've used all those pathetic
skinheads in the park.
Unbelievable. They think I'm
just as gullible as Gaia Moore.
They must think I'm the biggest
dunce in Rodke history.

Well, Skyler. . . Dad. . . I
think it's time I set the record
straight once and for all: You
have both underestimated the crap
out of me. You have no idea what
I am capable of. But I'm about to
show you. I don't even care about
your respect anymore. Because
I've lost all respect for you
both. In fact, you should both
feel free to hate me. And you are
going to hate me.

Because I'm about to blow your
entire operation sky-high. That
will be my greatest deed of all.
That will be God's greatest gift.
To screw you both to the wall.

GAIA KNEW NEXT TO NOTHING ABOUT

flirtation. And she knew even less about fake flirtation. This wasn't going to be easy. But she would try to look at it like a grueling final exam. Her last required high school course.

Fake Flirtation

Section II—Advanced Fake Flirtation

How to snow a man you despise using feminine sexuality and womanly wiles.

Final exam counts as one hundred percent of your grade.

Womanly wiles. What the hell did Gaia know about womanly wiles? Now would have been a good time to put in a call to Heather for her expertise. But there simply wasn't time. Gaia would have to wing it.

All she had to draw on were the behaviors she had witnessed in the past. It was a tendency she had always been ashamed of. Social voyeurism. She spent so much of her life isolated from the "cliques" of the world that she'd ended up simply observing their ways. The ways of the beautiful people. From her earliest days at the Village School, she'd caught herself staring at the FOHs in their fresh blowouts and couture, flirting with their leather-jacketed, trucker-capped male counterparts, milling about in the cafeteria or at Starbucks, engaging in their common teenage mating rituals. It wasn't very different from watching groups of monkeys at the zoo. A grab here, a hoot there, the occasional butt scratch. . .

But she'd at least picked up a few things in her observation.

There was the "incessant giggle," and there was the "hair flip." They were the most obvious female flirting maneuvers. Gaia sometimes wondered how Megan and Melanie didn't have sore necks and laryngitis after hair flipping and giggling their way through entire lunches with the boys. But far more effective than either of those classics was the all-powerful "arm grab."

Nothing seemed to telegraph a sexual invitation quite as clearly as a simple grabbing of the male arm. She had witnessed it a thousand times. She'd watched Megan work the captain of the football team, Rob Preston. She'd watched Rob's eyes light up the moment Megan grabbed his bicep while giggling at his joke about lunch meat. *Oh, yeah, game on,* his eyes seemed to say. *She wants it.*

The grabbing of the male bicep was equivalent to the stroking of his ego. And if Gaia knew anything about Skyler Rodke, it was that his ego liked to be stroked. He clearly got off on the domination—the power he still thought he had over her. So she would have to use that to her advantage. She swaddled herself in numbing emotional armor, and then she reached forward and grabbed his arm.

"I like this jacket," she said matter-of-factly, squeezing his arm and running her fingers along the fabric.

The grab seemed to induce the desired effect. Something in Skyler's eyes definitely changed. The remaining suspicion about Jake's message seemed to wane. She also noted an apparent "boy reflex." The moment she grabbed his arm, Skyler flexed his biceps ever so slightly. Was he even aware of it, or was it just his perpetual subconscious need to show off? Either way it was pathetic. But she knew she was on the right track. So she took the next step. It was really no different than a chess game, this whole flirtation thing. You always had to be planning at least three moves ahead.

She forced herself to cozy up closer to Skyler, squeezing both her hands around his strong arm and nestling her head on his shoulder.

"Hey," he uttered, with that same cuddly tone she'd foolishly bought into so many times before. He wrapped his arm around her shoulders and pulled the stray hairs behind her ear with his fingers. Her muscles threatened to tense with repulsion, but she kept them relaxed. This was, after all, the exact behavior she was trying to encourage. "Are you okay?" he asked.

"I don't know." She sighed, sliding her hand slowly down his arm and clasping her fingers in his. "I feel bad."

"Why?"

"About this whole Jake thing. I guess the prom is some kind of big deal to him. He was still so pissed in his message."

"Well, that's really his problem, not yours," Skyler said. "But if it's going to make you uncomfortable to see him there, we don't even have to go to the prom."

"No, I want to go."

"You do?" he asked quietly, leaning his face into hers. His lips grazed her forehead with each word. He ran his fingers gently through her hair. And that's when Gaia realized. . .

She was clearly not the only one flirting.

"Seriously, Gaia. Do you really want to go to the prom?" he asked, fondling her knee with his fingertips.

"Well, I want to go with *you*." She smiled, dabbing the tip of his nose with her index finger. She'd seen that one in some crappy movie somewhere.

"Hmmm. . . I don't know. . . ." Skyler smiled dubiously, sliding his own finger down the bridge of her nose. "You're not exactly the high-school-prom type." He laughed. "Aren't proms for people who actually *liked* high school? Who would you even want to see there? Not Jake. Not any of those girls you despise. What's the point?"

Gaia froze. His question had thrown her off balance. She was sitting there trying to play this flirtatious spy game, but out of complete nowhere he'd hit her with this wave of annoyingly *real* emotions. His question sent her flashing back through her time at the Village School and asking herself the very same question.

What exactly *was* the point of attending the prom? Or even graduation, for that matter? Every connection she had to the Village School had either disappeared or been damaged beyond repair. All of her potential happy endings had been canceled out one by one. There was a time when she could have imagined going to the prom with Sam. She'd pictured him at her graduation, sitting out in the audience next to her dad, applauding as she accepted her diploma, posing arm in arm with her—Gaia in her cap and gown—as her father snapped sunny pictures of them for the family album. But those images had all faded into oblivion a long time ago.

There was a time when she had imagined going to the prom with Mary. They would have been each other's dates, and Mary would have given her some hysterically slutty red Lycra dress to wear, and they would have spiked the punch with Ex-Lax and looked on with glee as the FOHs rushed desperately into the ladies' room one by one for the entire evening. But that future had died along with Mary.

And then, of course, there was Ed. That was the future that had seemed the most possible—the most certain: sitting next to him at graduation, holding hands under their gowns, waiting at her apartment to see what kind of delightfully cheesy surprise he'd have for her when he picked her up for the prom. . . another horse-driven carriage, perhaps? A two-seater bicycle. . . ?

That wasn't going to happen either.

She'd even managed to forge some kind of friendship with Heather in the end. But Heather was gone, too. And Gaia's friendship with Liz had hardly gotten a chance to turn into anything solid. Which left Jake as her only tenuous connection to that school.

Jake. Just what exactly was left of her connection with Jake? She wasn't even sure. She still had feelings for him, but he was so bound up with Oliver now. He'd gotten caught up in all the worst aspects of her life, and now. . .

Jesus, Gaia. Now. Come back to now, *for chrissake. Hellooo?*

She shook off her depressing trip down fantasy lane and forced herself to refocus on the matter at hand. And the matter at hand was, in fact, Jake.

Jake was the entire point of the current act she was putting on with Skyler. Because as much as she'd begun to lose her trust in him, she still believed that she owed Jake a call back after hearing his desperate message. She just wanted to let him know that there was no need to worry. She was well aware of the danger she was in, and she had the situation completely under control. But how exactly was she going to make that call with Skyler back on full-time watch? Answer: by shaking off her nasty bout with real emotions and getting back in touch with the fake ones. Otherwise her flirtatious snow job in progress would not only be repellent and nauseating. . . it would also be a complete waste of time.

So stop mourning the loss of your stupid high school happy endings. They're long since dead and buried.

Just get back to business. . . .

"MAYBE YOU'RE RIGHT." GAIA sighed, nuzzling her face deeper into Skyler's neck. "I don't think anyone really cares whether I show up at the prom or not. I was never really a part of that school. I was always just sort of passing through. I mean, forget about graduation—I never learned a thing at that place that I didn't know already. But I still might want to go to the prom. Just to piss them all off one last time." There was no need to lie about her end-of-the-year ambivalence. That would just complicate things further. But now it was time to start lying again.

"But the way I just dissed Jake to go with you," she moaned. "I still think it was kind of harsh."

Male Pride

52

"Oh, come on," Skyler said. "Jake will be fine. I bet he's got himself another date already."

"You're probably right," she lied. "But I don't want to leave this school feeling like a total bitch." *Too late for that.* "I just think I should at least call him back. I mean, you should have heard him, Skyler. He was *so* pissed at me."

"Well, why don't you let me call him?" Skyler suggested. "You know, we can have a little man-to-man. I'll be totally polite, I promise—"

"No way," Gaia jumped in. "That would just make things worse. No, I really think I need to be the one to make the call." She slid her hand slowly under Skyler's jacket and grabbed firmly to his waist. "It's a scary call to make, but I think I can do it." She ran her fingers gently along his muscular torso. "Is that cool with you. . . ?"

Skyler looked deep into her fake doe eyes. "Of course." He smiled, brushing her forehead with a kiss. "If you want to call him, I totally understand. And don't be scared. I'll be right here if it gets ugly."

Oh, that's so comforting, Skyler. Don't worry. I'm not scared.

"You're the best." She smiled back, giving him a peck on the cheek. *Note to self: Wash lips ASAP.*

Gaia pulled her cell phone back out of her pocket and dialed Jake's number. She looked back at Skyler and faked a fearful cringe as she listened to the phone ring.

Okay. Here goes. . . . Be smart, Jake. Please be smart about this phone call. . . .

Jake picked up on the second ring. "Thank God!" he shouted far too loudly. "What the hell took you so long?"

Gaia slammed her finger on the volume button and took it down as far as she could, glancing back at Skyler's watchful eyes.

"Calm down, Jake," she insisted.

"Calm down?" Jake squawked. "Are you kidding me? Did you get my message? Did you hear what I—?"

"*Yes*, I got your message. And I know how upset you are about the *prom*."

Jake went silent. She could feel his confusion pouring through the phone line. *Come on, Jake. Work with me here. Figure it out. . . .*

"The prom?" Jake asked. "What the hell are you talking about? Forget about the prom—did you hear what I said about Chris and Skyler? About the whole Rodke—?"

"Yes, I *heard* everything you said," she interrupted. Now she tried to pronounce each word as deliberately as possible, hoping Jake would get the picture. "I heard everything you said, and I *know*, okay? I *know* what the situation is. But you shouldn't be upset, because I know what I'm doing. I'm going to the prom with Skyler. Not you. Okay? Deal with it."

She glanced at Skyler, who gave her an encouraging thumbs-up. What an ass.

"Gaia, why the hell are we talking about the *prom*?"

54

Jake's frustration was building. "We already agreed we were going to the prom."

"Yes, we did, didn't we? Good point."

Jake paused. "What?"

"Uh-huh. . . Uh-huh. . . No, I've made my decision. I'm sorry."

"Wait. . . what? Gaia, what the hell are you talking about?"

Jesus, Jake. Haven't you ever had a coded conversation before? Pick up the goddamn signals. "Well, I just don't agree with that, Jake, that's all. I think you need to get over it."

"Wait a minute." Jake paused. "Gaia. . . Is he there right now?"

"Yes," she groaned. *Finally. It took you long enough.* She rolled her eyes to Skyler. "Yes, Jake. You're a smart guy. And you're a good-looking guy, and I know you'll find another date. I really hope everything works out for you. And I'm sorry. But you'll be fine, and *I will be fine*. I am *fine*. Are we clear?"

"All right, Gaia, listen to me," Jake ordered. "I'll do the talking, okay? You just answer yes or no. Are you in danger right now?"

No, this was the last thing she needed. She just wanted Jake to know that she'd gotten his message—that she had things under control. This conversation couldn't go on too long or Skyler would start getting suspicious again.

"Gaia?" Jake called out. "Gaia, can you hear me? Are you being held hostage? Are you in danger?"

"No." She sighed. "Look, Jake, I don't want to talk anymore, all right? I just wanted you to know—"

"Tell us where you are. We can have people there in two minutes."

"No."

"*What? Just tell* us where you are so we can—"

"Jake, *no.* You're not *listening* to me." She threw up her arms to Skyler with fake frustration. Though her frustration wasn't really so fake. Jake needed to understand her position here. She had to punch up the key phrases to give him the message. "You have to *listen* to me, Jake, all right? Look, I'm sick of arguing with you. We don't need to argue anymore because *I know what I'm doing.* Do you understand? *I've got it under control.* I know you're upset, but this really doesn't concern you anymore. *I don't want you involved.* I can take care of myself. I can make my own choices. And I'm going with Skyler."

"Don't do this," Jake insisted. "I know what you're trying to do, but don't be an idiot. Don't try to handle this whole thing alone."

"Jake, I really have to go now, okay? So find yourself another date."

"*No.* Do *not* hang up, Gaia. Don't—"

There was suddenly loud rustling on the other end of the line, and then there was a new voice on the phone. A much angrier voice that Gaia did not remotely want to hear.

"Gaia, it's Oliver. What the hell are you doing? Tell me where you are *now.*"

"I have to go," Gaia said coldly.

"Goddammit! Don't you hang up that phone!"

The look in Skyler's eyes began to shift and Gaia could see it. The slightest hint of suspicion. He could hear the yelling. He could tell something was wrong. "What is Jake's problem?" he complained. "This is ridiculous. Let me talk to him." He reached his hand for the phone.

"No," Gaia whispered, swiping Skyler's hand away. "It's *fine.*"

"Gaia?" Oliver barked. "Gaia, is that him? Is that that Rodke boy? Put that son of a bitch on the phone."

"Just give me the phone," Skyler complained. "What is wrong with that asshole? I'll take care of this."

Gaia shoved his hand away again. "Look, this conversation is over!" Gaia shouted into the phone. "I'm hanging up."

"Gaia—"

She slammed her thumb down on the disconnect button just as Skyler finally managed to grab the phone from her.

"Listen to me, Jake," Skyler hissed into the phone. "She's going with me. What's done is done, dude. Get the hell over it, all right? Hello. . . ? *Hello?*" Skyler looked over at Gaia.

"He hung up," she explained.

"God, what*ever*." Skyler snorted, throwing the phone down on the couch. "Thank God you're not going with him. That kid's a freaking psycho. Was someone else on the phone, too? I thought I heard someone else."

"Jake's dad," Gaia replied, thinking on her feet. "He picked up, too. Now his whole family hates my guts."

Skyler rolled his eyes. "It's just a *prom date,* people. They should get some family therapy."

"Don't I know it," Gaia mumbled. "Ugh, I'm just glad that's over with." She pasted a troubled expression on her face and quickly crawled back into Skyler's arms, praying that would once again work its distractive magic. "I'm just glad you're here," she added with as much baby-talk flavor as she could muster.

Thankfully, it seemed to work. Skyler took a relaxing breath and wrapped his arm back around Gaia's shoulders. "I'm here," he assured her, giving her another kiss on the head. "Man, doesn't Jake have any pride? What a loser."

The irony of that statement was almost too much to take. Jake had plenty of pride. Too much pride. Along with Oliver, and Skyler, and Chris, and just about every other man she'd ever met. This little phone call was just a microcosm of her entire experience with men. All she'd wanted to do was make contact with Jake and put his mind at ease. But what had she ended up with? All of these men shouting at her or pawing for her phone, just dying to do battle with each other. All of these men assuming that she was utterly incapable of taking care of herself—of solving her own problems. What the hell was the matter with men? **What were all the mothers and fathers of this world doing wrong with their baby boys?** Because as far as Gaia could tell, money wasn't the root of all evil. Male pride was. Not that she could necessarily speak for the rest of the world. But as far as she was concerned, male pride had been decimating her life since she was six years old. And someday it would surely be the death of her. Somehow that seemed inevitable.

When she
thought about
all those boys
now, they all
seemed **spewing**
like such
testosterone
shallow,
materialistic,
immature
tools.

"GET ME GENERAL COLTER ON THE

Idiot Child

line. *Now.*"

"Yes, sir, and who should I say is calling, sir?"

"You tell him this is Robert Rodke. Tell him it's urgent. I need him on the line *pronto*."

"Of course, sir, yes, sir, please hold."

Chris had to stifle a giggle. He felt like he was right smack in the middle of one of those huge, crappy Michael Bay blockbusters, and he was loving every minute of it. *"Get me General Colter on the line."* It was just the kind of line Chris had always been dying to say. That and the word *pronto*. There couldn't possibly be anyone in real life who said *pronto*. It was almost as good as *"Get me the president!"* He could just picture those military drones on the other end of the line, rushing around to find the general based solely on Chris's demand. He could picture the general marching through some office filled with American flags and picking up the red phone. Of course, it probably wasn't red, but this was Chris's movie now, and in his movie the phone was red.

He'd gotten Colter's classified phone number right off the "classified" contract—a little less "classified" now that Chris had seen it. All he'd had to do was dial, speak, and wait. So freaking easy. . .

"This is Colter," the brusque voice finally barked through the phone.

"Yes, is this General John T. Colter?"

"Speaking. Rodke. . . ?"

"Yes," Chris said.

"This is Robert Rodke?" The general sounded unconvinced.

"Well. . . no. This is Chris Rodke, actually. I just needed you to take the call. We met earlier today. . . ?"

Dead silence on the line. Chris had expected as much, but it was only a matter of time before he'd have the general listening.

"How the hell did you get this number?" Colter asked.

"That really doesn't matter, General. What matters is the information I am about to give you."

"Listen, boy. . ." Colter's western drawl seemed to grow with each dismissive word. "I don't know how you got this number, but I don't have any time for crank calls, you understand? Don't you call this number again—"

"This is no crank call, General. This is, in fact, a deadly serious call, and I suggest you listen, because once you hear what I have to say, you will be thinking very differently about the deal you are about to make with my father's company."

"And what the hell would you know about that?"

"What would I know, General? I'd know *a lot*. A hell of a lot more than you know, that's for sure. And given that you haven't hung up yet, I know you're going to listen. So here's a refreshing dose of *truth* for you, General. . . . That drug my father is trying to sell you—it's a lemon. It's damaged goods. Not only is it *not* what you signed up for, but it is something much, much worse. And I just thought you'd like to hear a few examples of—"

"Get to the goddamn point."

"Sir, yes, sir," Chris replied sarcastically. "The point is that the drug you are about to give to your soldiers is a complete and utter disaster. It does not work. It has *major* side effects, including uncontrollable mania, brutally violent tendencies—not to mention the fact that it seems to be one hundred percent addictive. If you make this deal, you will be making the biggest mistake of your military career. Of your life, actually."

"This is a joke. I'm not about to take advice from some teenage kid. If you've got issues with your daddy, then you can take them elsewhere, son. Find yourself a good shrink and don't ever—"

"General, have you by chance been reading the New York papers? Do the words *Invince* or *Droogs,* or *ultraviolence* mean anything to you? Because if you'd been keeping up on your current events, then you'd know how serious this is, and you would *stop* talking to me like some idiot *child.* I am telling you, my father and my brother are trying to snow you. They just want to make the deal, no matter what the cost. But I have

63

been out there on the streets, General. I have seen what this stuff does to people, and unless you want an army full of stark-raving-mad trainees murdering each other on Base 9 and wreaking havoc through the entire Republic of Congo, you will shut up and listen to me."

Colter was silent. He must not have expected Chris to be so well informed. Now he was listening.

"I figured you'd have your doubts," Chris went on, "so I'm going to make it very easy for you. I'm going to give you a demonstration of exactly what this stuff does to people. Tonight. Nine o'clock. In the lot on the corner of West Twelfth Street and the highway. You get your people down there. I will have administered doses of the drug to a group of boys not much younger than your trainees, and you just watch how they react. You watch and see what people hyped up on this drug will do to a man, and *then* you tell me just how much you want to buy it. I think you'll find yourself quite enlightened about the scam my family is trying to pull on you."

"Now, you listen to me, boy—"

"We're done here. Nine o'clock. West Twelfth and the highway. You can't possibly be stupid enough to ignore this warning. And if you are, then I promise you, it will be your loss. And the loss of all your men once they've ripped each other's throats out and shot each other to pieces. That is all."

Click.

Chris's pulse was racing double time. The blood was rushing through his head, pounding with every heartbeat. All things considered, he thought he had handled that rather beautifully. The general would see the carnage of the Droogs, and this whole operation would go up in smoke. Which left only one remaining problem.

Once his family's operation was exposed, Chris had to be damn sure that he didn't go down with them. He was sure he could play the innocent little brother through any amount of police questioning. It was his word against his corrupt family's, and he, after all, was the good-hearted young man who had exposed them. There was still just one little fly in the ointment. One nosy little spy boy who had witnessed Chris's involvement in the whole operation. For Chris to be completely in the clear, that little problem would have to be dealt with.

So now it was time to kill two birds with one stone. Chris picked up the phone again and dialed the main number for the Village School. . . .

"Village School, how may I help you?" Ms. Kimball's precious little schoolmarm voice was such a welcome departure from the general's testosto-speak.

"Yes, hiii," Chris crooned. "This is Chris Rodke. . . ."

"*Yes,* hello, Chris. Oh gosh, I hope you're feeling better."

"I am feeling a little better, thanks, Ms. Kimball. But I was supposed to get some homework assignments from Jake Montone. Would you happen to have his number?"

"Of course, Chris, you just hold on one sec, okay?"

"Oh, *thank you*."

Yes, all things considered, his plan was moving along quite beautifully.

HEATHER WAS COUCHED DEEP IN A

chair in the telephone room. Her legs and arms were folded tightly as she stared at the blurry telephone, trying to work up the courage to pick it up and make the call.

Blind Date

It shouldn't have been a scary call to make, but somehow she was still nervous. She'd already been rejected by Ed, and she wasn't in the mood for more. But she ran a much bigger risk of rejection by calling this particular boy. After all, he'd rejected her in the worst possible way a very long time ago. He'd dumped her for another girl. But so much time had passed since then. And now, for some reason, he was the one she really wanted to call.

She'd already considered every other option. She'd considered asking one of her old Village School classmates, but, as she and Ed had discussed, she'd changed so much since then. When she thought about those boys now, they all seemed like such shallow, materialistic, immature tools. Besides, they had all surely paired off with her friends by now.

She'd thought about asking one of the guys at Carverton to be her escort, but that just didn't seem fair. For one thing, he'd be forced to sit through some prom he couldn't have cared less about, and worse than that, he'd probably end up being a spectacle for all her haughty friends to judge. She could hear the whispered jokes already. . . . *Oh, look, Heather brought a blind date. Get it? Blind date?* Ha ha. Real mature, girls. No, Heather wasn't about to subject a Carverton boy to that kind of hell.

The more she had thought it through, there was really only one other boy she'd wanted to ask besides Ed. She wanted a date who could give her the feeling that she'd come full circle—that she'd truly come back. She wanted a date who would make her feel like her old self again. Well. . . her old self *minus* all the `shallow, catty tendencies that had turned her into such a raving queen bitch`. She wanted to feel like a queen again—just minus the bitch part. Maybe she even wanted to prove to him that she had successfully exorcised her inner bitch—that she had finally grown up. Wasn't that what graduations and proms were all about?

So she'd made a bunch of calls to finally get his

number. She just needed to pick up the damn phone and dial it.

Just do it. Call him. What do you have to lose? The worst he can say is no. He won't be mean about it or anything. He never had a mean bone in his body. Besides, you're still Heather Gannis, for God's sake. This should be a walk in the park.

Finally, after five more minutes of embarrassing hesitation, she breathed in and picked up the phone, dialing the number ever so slowly and then waiting. Her heart began to pound, and her palms began to sweat, and she did seriously consider hanging up at least four times within the three rings. But once she'd heard his sweet, raspy voice, it was too late.

"Hello?"

Heather went silent.

"Hello?" he repeated.

Now's the time when you talk, Heather. TALK.

"Hel-*looo?*" he groaned. Two more seconds and he was going to hang up. It was do-or-die time. . . .

"Sam?"

"Yeah. . . Who's this?"

Who's this? Doesn't he even remember my voice? Has it been that long?

"It's *Heather*," she said, trying to mask her embarrassment with a laugh.

"Oh God, *Heather*, I'm so sorry." Sam laughed, too.

"I didn't even recognize your voice. Wow. . ." Suddenly he sounded much more serious. "Heather. . . How *are* you?"

"How am I?" It seemed like a more complicated question than it should have been. "I'm. . . I'm okay. I am truly okay, Sam. How are you?"

Sam seemed to have to pause and think about it, too. "I'm okay, too," he said thoughtfully.

"Well, *okay*." She tried to take in some good breaths. "So I guess we're both okay."

"I guess we are," Sam said quietly. "Who would have thought it?"

It was already so much more awkward than she'd expected. Awkward but somehow. . . nice. Something about hearing Sam's voice made her feel happier and more nervous at the same time. Which, she supposed, was how he'd always made her feel. Giddy but insecure.

"Well, Sam, for both of our sakes, I'm just going to get right to the point."

"Okay. . . ?" He sounded a wee bit scared.

"Don't worry," she assured him. "It's nothing bad."

"Oh, good," he said. "I've lost all capacity for bad news. I kind of reached my quota, you know?"

"Tell me about it. No, it's not bad. I mean, I *hope* it's not bad to you. I mean, I guess you could see it as bad, but I'd hoped you wouldn't because. . . Ugh. Listen to me. I feel like I'm twelve."

"Heather," he said in a calming tone. "What's up?"

"Right. Sorry. I'll get back to the point. The *point* is that, you know. . . I'm graduating."

"I know. You guys have made it through. Congratulations."

"Yes, thanks. I must say, it wasn't as easy as it was supposed to be. But that's still not the point."

"I didn't think so."

"No. . . Nope. No, the point is. . ." *Breathe, Heather. If this is your "grown-up" behavior, you've got a hell of a ways to go.* "Sorry. Okay. The point is, when we graduate, we also have this one last high school ritual known as The Prom."

"Yes. I am familiar with this ritual."

"Right." Heather laughed. "And I'm kind of coming into this whole prom thing a little late. And the point is. . . well. . . I need a date."

"Aha. I see. . . ." Sam went silent. Heather's mouth went so dry, she couldn't unglue her lips from her teeth. "Well," Sam said, "I mean. . . I'm sure I know a few guys."

There was a long silence on the line.

"Oh. . ." The air seeped out of Heather's lungs. Rejection number two. Her chest began to hurt. Her eyes stung from trying to fight off unexpected tears. "Well. . . yeah," she uttered, trying to keep her voice from quavering with disappointment. "If, uh. . . If you know someone who'd be willing to take me—"

"Heather."

"What?"

"I'm kidding."

"You are?"

"Are you asking me to the prom?"

"I was, yes," she replied meekly.

"Well, I would be honored," he said. Now she could hear his devastating smile over the phone.

She literally fell back in her chair, slapping her hand over her head with relief. The smile spread so wide over her face, it almost hurt. One of those tears she'd been fighting off managed to escape from the corner of her eye.

"Heather, why didn't you just ask me in the first place?"

"I don't *know*," she said, laughing out all her pent-up nerves. "I mean, after everything we'd been through, I didn't even know if you'd want to talk to me. I was afraid you'd say no."

"Well, you were wrong. I think we've both been through enough rejection, don't you?"

"Amen, Sam." Heather sighed. "A-freaking-men to that."

"One thing, though," Sam said. "Um. . . is Gaia going to be there?"

The emotional roller coaster continued. Here they were at the very end of the school year, and they were still talking about Gaia

Moore. Boy, did that bring back a ton of ugly flash-backs. "To be honest, I don't know," she said. "Why?" She clenched her teeth. "Is that going to be a problem for you? If she's there?"

Sam took far too long to answer this. But he did finally answer. "No," he said. "No, that won't be a problem for me." It sounded like he was discovering this fact for the very first time. But it also sounded like he was pretty happy with his discovery. And that made Heather happy.

"Well, good." She smiled.

"You know, Gaia wasn't the only major relation-ship in my life. I seem to remember you and I having a good thing. You know. . . before."

"Yeah," Heather breathed. "I remember." She felt herself fading back into fond memories of her and Sam Moon: at restaurants. . . in Sheep Meadow in the park. . . in bed. . .

She quickly thrust herself back into the present. "But I'm not—I mean, this prom deal is a purely pla-tonic request."

"Oh, *hell*, yes." Sam laughed. "I'm not crazy enough to try that again. I mean. . . no offense."

"None taken," she assured him. "But I'm not that girl anymore, Sam. I swear I'm not."

"You know what?" he said. "I can tell."

That might very well be the sweetest thing he'd ever said to her. No, maybe not the sweetest. But it was the thing she had most wanted to hear from him. She knew she had made the right call. There truly was only one Sam Moon.

NOW JAKE WAS THE ONE PACING THE

Evil Pills

floor. Oliver was just sitting there on the couch, brooding.

That agonizing coded phone call had pushed his blood pressure to its absolute maximum. Why did she even call if she wasn't going to let him help? Was she *trying* to get herself killed? Was that what was happening here? Because that was the only possible explanation for her denying his help and staying put in that apartment with Skyler Rodke. The girl had to be suicidal.

Jake finally stopped his pacing and turned to Oliver. "So what do we do now?"

Oliver didn't answer. He just sat there burning a hole into the opposite wall with his eyes.

"Oliver? What do we do now?"

Oliver didn't even turn to look at him. "We find Chris Rodke."

"How? You said it yourself. The asshole is hiding. Even your crack staff can't find the kid—"

"Shut up," Oliver snapped. He flashed Jake a venomous glance. "Just keep your mouth shut and let me think."

"Okay. I'm sorry. I just don't see how we're going to find him. And I think we're running out of time. I think whatever they're going to do to her, it's going to—"

"I do *not* need your speculation, Jake. I do not need anything from you except *silence,* do you understand?"

Jake stomped his foot on the floor. "Look, what is *wrong* with you? What is with the way you've been talking to me? What is with the psychotic looks? I mean, I'm just as pissed as you are, but I thought we were in this together. I've never seen you like this. It's like you dropped some freaking 'evil pills' this morning or something. The *Rodkes* are the bad guys, remember? Not me, not you. *Them.*"

"I am becoming impatient." Oliver's jaw was practically sealed shut. It was a wonder he could form any words. "That is what is wrong with me. I am losing patience." He stood up from the couch and began to walk toward Jake with a near-menacing glare. "And you're right, Jake. You are not my son. You could not possibly *be* my son, because no son of mine would ever allow himself to be spotted by his *mark.* No son of mine would be talking to me with such *disrespect.*"

Jake was beginning to feel a little nervous. Despite

everything he knew about Oliver, he was honestly getting a little scared. And Jake wasn't generally one to get scared. But the closer Oliver got, the more Jake was compelled to move away.

"Okay," Jake uttered, holding out his hands. "All right, I'm sorry. Just calm down, okay?"

But Oliver didn't stop advancing. "No, it is not okay. Nothing about this situation is okay. You have obviously lost Gaia's trust. And you have lost us Chris Rodke. You have lost us everything, Jake. Every card we had to play. And I am beginning to think that you are not necessary to this op—"

Jake's cell phone suddenly rang. It froze them both in place as the shrill ring echoed off the high ceilings and the oversized windows. Whoever it was—Gaia, or his dad, or even a wrong number—Jake was relieved. He honestly didn't know what Oliver would have done if he'd come any closer.

Jake pulled his phone from his pocket. He didn't recognize the number, but he flipped open the phone immediately. Anything to defuse the mounting tension in the room. "Hello?"

"Jake?"

"Yeah?"

"It's Chris."

Jake nearly dropped the phone. His spine went stiff as he widened his eyes to Oliver. "Chris. . . ," he breathed.

Even Oliver's cold eyes widened with surprise. He frantically began mouthing a word that Jake couldn't understand until the third try.

"*Number*," he was whispering.

Jake grabbed a pen from the kitchen counter and scrawled down the cell number that had shown up on his phone. Oliver ripped the piece of paper from the pad and rushed to his laptop. He was obviously going to try and trace the call. But Jake was nowhere near that kind of clearheaded action. He could still hardly move. He could still hardly believe that the guy he'd been so desperate to find had called *him*.

"Surprised?" Chris asked. Even a one-word sentence from this kid's mouth was smarmy as hell.

"Surprised," Jake repeated. "Yeah."

"Surprised by the call or by seeing me in the park?"

"Both," Jake replied.

Jesus. That answered that question. Zan was right. Chris had seen him there. That drug-addled mess of a girl was right. Jake felt sick to his stomach.

He could feel his anger welling up in his chest. The shock of the call began to wear off. He had Chris Rodke on the phone—'*God*,'—the guy who'd been dealing Invince to the scum of the earth, the reason for Jake's near-death experiences in the park, the reason for Gaia's near-death experiences past, present, and quite possibly future. The cocky son of a bitch sounded positively *pleasant*. Jake wished there was some way to reach right through that phone and wrap his hands around the asshole's neck. But all Jake could use were his words—his least favorite weapon by far. He pressed the phone hard to his face. "Where is she?" he demanded. "Where's Gaia? She's somewhere with your scumbag brother. Where? What is your sick-ass family planning? How is she involved. . . ?"

"*Whoa, whoa, whoa,* there. Slow *down,* Jake. One question at a time."

"Answer them *all,* Chris. Answer every goddamn question, or I swear to God—"

"You swear to God *what?* What will you do, Jake? Jesus, you sound just like my father."

"Shut *up* and answer the question."

"Jake, you're contradicting yourself. Do you want me to shut up or answer the question? I honestly can't do both."

Jake wanted something to pound so bad. He wanted something to put his fist through—something to substitute for Chris Rodke's face. But he had to keep it together. He had no choice. "Listen to me, Chris. Just tell me where Gaia is. That's it. Because if you don't tell me where she is, then when I *do* find you, I swear to God I am going to pound your face in so freaking hard—"

"Jake. . . I'm sorry to interrupt, but does this macho crap work with the ladies? Because it's really not doing it for me."

Jake was about to internally combust. "Is this *funny* to you?" he hollered. "Is it really funny to you to make me suffer? And Gaia and every other totally innocent kid that your IV-heads have maimed? Does your family just sit down to dinner and have a big laugh about all the lives you're destroying?"

"No, none of this is funny to me!" Chris shouted. "Not in the least. And if you could stop thumping your chest and howling like an ape long enough to *listen* to me, you might actually discover that we both feel pretty much the *same way.*"

"What are you talking about?"

"We both hate my brother. And we both hate my father. And we'd both like to see their entire plan get burned to the ground." Chris paused for dramatic effect. "Do I have your attention now? Or would you rather keep spewing testosterone at me?"

Jake finally fell silent. His eyes met with Oliver's, and then he turned his attention back to the phone. This time he spoke at a much lower volume. "I'm listening," he mumbled.

"Listening!" Chris celebrated. "What a novel idea. Let's stick with that plan, Jake. *You* listen and *I* talk. I think you'll far prefer the results. So, here's the deal. You and I will meet tonight at nine o'clock, in the empty lot on the corner of West Twelfth Street and the highway. And I will tell you absolutely everything I know. About Gaia, about the entire operation, *everything*. And then we will go our separate ways. And that will be that. Simple. Agreed?"

Jake was still trying to catch up. He couldn't even tell which side Chris was on now. But he knew he was in no position to bargain right now. "Fine," he said. "I'll be there."

"*Just* you and me, Jake," Chris stressed. "You will come alone, or you will most definitely *not* see or hear from me again. Understood?"

Jake could practically feel his tail tucked between his legs. It was infuriating. "Understood."

"*Good.* Then goodbye."

The call was dropped. Jake just stood there in a mild state of shock. He finally turned to Oliver. "He hung up."

"*Damn* it!" Oliver shouted. "We couldn't finish the trace."

"We don't need the trace," Jake said. "He's meeting me. Tonight at nine. He says I have to come alone, or he won't show."

Oliver finally looked half calm for a moment. "Well, then we'll just have to make damn sure he believes that you're alone."

Their voices
started to
meld into a
hellish **last**
chorus **goodbye**
of deafening
noise.

Catty Bitch Fever

OF COURSE, THEY WOULD HAVE TO BE here. Ed should have expected it. He'd been out on a long walk, trying to keep his mind off the supreme anticlimax that would be the prom. But he'd apparently cleared his head of all common sense and made the foolish decision to duck into the Astor Place Starbucks for an evening hot chocolate.

The Astor Place Starbucks. A home away from home for the FOHs.

What were you thinking, Fargo? What the hell were you thinking?

Simple. He hadn't been thinking. And now he found himself right smack in the middle of a late-evening prom chat-a-thon of biblical proportions. Megan, Tammie, Laurie, Melanie, Trish—an entire gaggle of FOHs were sitting there holding forth on their favorite topic. And they weren't just holding forth: they were holding forth while tweaked out of their minds on God knew how many caramel Frappuccinos.

"Okay," Megan said. "Not that it's a contest, but who do you think ended up with the best dress?"

"I'd say it's between you and Tammie," Laurie said. "But only because of the shoes. I am totally willing to confess shoe envy."

"Century 21," Megan said, shrugging as if to say, *Who knew?*

"I still can't believe that," Melanie chimed in.

"Neither could *I*," Megan squeaked. "I never thought I'd match the color. It was like the prom gods had just put them there for me. I swear they were just sitting there on the shelf, glowing. I heard angels singing."

Run, Ed. Run for your life.

Ed tried to duck and cover, but they'd already spotted him.

"*Ed*," they howled in unison. He cringed.

"Come sit with us," Tammie insisted.

"I really can't. I've got to—"

"*Sit*," Melanie commanded, jumping up from her seat and tugging him over by the arm. "This is end-of-high-school *bonding*, Ed. This is the time of the year when we all realize just how much we actually loved each other, so you can't say no. It's a scientific imperative."

Ed wasn't aware of this scientific imperative. And he certainly hadn't yet realized how much he loved the FOHs. But he was trapped. He opted to stand rather than sit, hoping he would find a polite exit within the next minute. But that didn't seem good enough for them.

Melanie put her hands on her hips and stared at Ed accusingly. "Ed. Come on. What's with the frown? Don't tell me you and Kai aren't super-psyched for prom."

"Okay, I won't tell you."

"Ed, come *on*," Megan groaned. "It's all over! This is it. The end of our high school careers. The grand finale. So show me some love." She spread her arms wide open for a hug.

Ed bowed his head. He was hoping he looked more embarrassed than annoyed, but it was no use. The whole group closed in on him, coaxing him along with shouts of, "Come on, Ed, show us some *love*." They ultimately pushed him into the middle of a massive FOH group hug. The flood of conflicting designer fragrances nearly cut off his oxygen. Now he could only pray they wouldn't start singing that Celine Dion song from *Titanic*.

They finally released him from the hug, but now he was surrounded. They'd left him with no escape route and immediately picked up their chat-a-thon right where they'd left off.

"Okay, okay," Laurie announced excitedly. "We all agree, Megan wins best dress. But here's a better one. . . . Who's going to win *worst* dress?"

They all shared knowing glances as if the answer was so obvious, there was no need to ask it.

"Um, can you say 'Gaia'?" Megan giggled. They all shared a hearty Frappuccino-induced laugh.

"I *can*, I just don't want to," Tammie joked. "Okay, here's what I'm picturing. . . . " She placed her hand over her eyes like a psychic medium. "I see a black potato-sack-like funeral dress. . . very JC Penney. . . . I see a `dirty gray sweatshirt` zipped over the dress, and the shoes. . . the shoes will be. . ."

"Cleats," Laurie said.

"*Yes*," Tammie guffawed. "Yes. Those black cleats with the white stripes!"

"They were the only black shoes she had!" Megan announced, providing them all with their punch line.

Ed's head began to ache with a terrible case of catty bitch fever. It was time to go.

"Ladies," he announced, "so sorry to cut this end-of-the-year 'love fest' short, but I'm late for something or other."

Ed turned around, but Melanie grabbed hold of his arm again. "*Okay*, Ed." She sighed. "Sorry. We won't be mean anymore, okay? Promise."

"No, I really do have to go—"

"Come *on*. We get it. Gaia's a sore topic for you. We weren't thinking."

Ed resisted the strong impulse to pour scalding hot chocolate on Melanie. "What are you talking about?" he asked calmly. "Gaia's not a sore topic. Why would she be a sore topic?"

"Oh, come on," Laurie said. "I mean, I know you're the world's most laid-back guy, but don't tell me you're not a little jealous of Jake. Or is it *Skyler*. . . ?"

This question elicited a chorus of dark "ooh"s and "aah"s from the peanut gallery.

"I don't *knooow*. . . ." Tammie's eyes were blazing with gossipy fervor. "Am I the only one who noticed that Gaia and Jake were *both* absent from school today? Perhaps they were up all night fighting on the phone about a certain society boy. . . ?"

"Uch, I don't even *care* anymore," Megan moaned. "How much do you want to bet she doesn't even show up to prom at all?"

"I'm praying for it," Laurie said. "You know what? Honestly, I don't think anyone's even going to notice whether she's there or not."

"*Word*," Megan said. "Ladies, at the risk of tooting our own horns, I think it's safe to say that the most noticeable thing about this prom. . . will be our collective fabulousness."

They let out another excruciating group laugh, although as far as Ed could tell, Megan was barely even joking.

"Ed?" She giggled. "Do you concur?'

"Oh, absolutely," Ed said in a monotone. "Fabulous. No doubt about it."

"Wait, I'm having another vision!" Tammie announced. She placed her hand over her eyes again. "I see the five of us on prom night. . . stepping out of our limo with our gorgeous dates. . . decked out head to toe in stunning couture. . . . I see us stepping through the doors of the Supper Club like rock stars, doing our best supermodel struts. . . . I see all heads turning our way. . . . And then. . . I see us dancing our asses off. Because high school is *over*. . . .And *we*, dear ladies. . . are the *shiznit*. We *rule* the freakin' *school!*"

"Oh, that's fo' shizzle, my sizzle!"

The girls all broke into a caffeinated chorus of *TRL*-like *"woo-hoos,"* which dissolved into deafening waves of hearty laughter as they fell back in their chairs.

Ed could only stand and stare at this horrific display, thinking one thing:

That he yearned to reach the high school finish line.

And if the girls in college were anything like this. . . he was going straight to trade school.

People really are dying for
inspiration these days.
Inspiration of any kind. They
don't even seem to care if
they're being inspired to do
"good" or "bad," just as long as
they're being inspired. That's
why all the pathetic nonentities
of the world adore me so much.
That's why they take all the
pills I give them and do what I
tell them to do. Because I give
them these delicious doses of
artificial pride where there was
nothing but self-hatred. I fill
their lives with meaning where
there was nothing but emptiness.
It's like an unspoken pact of
sorts.

   A covenant.

   They worship me and they obey
my commandments, and in exchange
I show them glimpses of the
promised land. A land where there
will be no fear and no pain.
Where they'll finally be invinci-
ble. Of course, they'll never
actually *get* to that promised

land, but they don't really need to know that, do they? They don't even want to know that. It's the promise that keeps them coming back for more. It's the promise that keeps them following my commandments.

I suppose I have a bit of a Messiah complex. But what can I say? If it works for them, it works for me.

And besides, my father *has* forsaken me, right? There has to be some reason for that—some cosmic purpose. Otherwise what is the point of all of this?

I just came back from a meeting with my disciples. I handed each one of them a little orange glimpse of the promised land, and then I told them that if they followed my commandments for this evening, there would be much, much more where that came from. I offered them great rewards in exchange for one simple deed. It is most definitely an "evil deed," but that didn't seem to make much difference to them—they were quite happy to do it all the same. In fact, they seemed positively inspired to do it. Like I said, the "good" and "evil" part doesn't seem to make all that much difference to people. Just as long they're inspired.

It's funny, actually. Our little meeting got me to thinking about this country's rich history of religious cults and serial killers. So many of them have explained away their murders with the same old excuse:

God told me to do it. I was just obeying the word of God.

It seems like such a cop-out, doesn't it? It sounds like a lie. I mean, really, what are the odds that those psycho-killers got any real face time with the man upstairs? But in this one rare case, it will actually be the truth. They can blame the murder on God.

Because I *did* tell them to do it.

GAIA AND SKYLER HAD JUST FINISHED
watching *On the Waterfront*, the
last installment of their Brando
film festival. She had, of course,
paid no attention to the film
whatsoever. She'd only sat there
cuddled up with Skyler for two
reasons:

Rodke Hypnosis

1. To soften him up that much further with a host
   of gentle caresses and flirtatious tickles. And. . .
2. To place a nice long break between her calculated moves. Too much manipulation in one
   sitting would be too obvious.

Now she realized just how deeply insulting this
whole movie-watching MO of Skyler's was. It was
nothing more than a classic babysitting maneuver.
Put the baby in front of the idiot box and
the baby will stay silent, still, and subdued for hours.
No tantrums, no questions, no "trouble." It was just
another form of Rodke hypnosis.

*Watch the moving pictures on the big box, baby
Gaia. Aren't they pretty? Don't they make you want to
sit here and think about nothing for hours and hours?
Good. Because we don't want you to think. The last
thing we want you to do is think.*

But this time all she had done was think. Think

and think about her next move. She needed proof. She needed cold hard evidence of their plans. She had already found that small batch of research files in Skyler's "roommate's" desk. But there was nothing literal enough in those files to convict anyone of anything. There was no specific mention of Gaia's name or of what they were actually planning. And Gaia could think of only one other potential source of hard evidence in this prison of an apartment. But to get to it, there would have to be some more sucking up and some more lying. And the time was now.

Skyler flipped off the TV and took a long, luxurious stretch on the couch. Gaia took this opportunity to lie down in his lap. If that didn't scream "sexual tension," she didn't know what did. He looked down at her and smiled, placing his hand on her forehead and running his fingers through her hair.

"Wasn't that awesome?" he said. "Is Brando not the man?"

Gaia didn't answer. She was waiting for him to notice the angry expression she had now placed on her face. Which he did.

"What's wrong?"

"I'm sorry." She sighed. "Yes, the movie was awesome, but I'm still just so pissed at *Jake*. I mean, I was nice enough to call him back, and I tried to be polite about the whole prom thing, and he was *still* such a jerk about it."

"I know," Skyler agreed. "What a freak. You'd think he'd never gotten dissed before."

"Yeah. I can't believe I ever spent any time with that guy. It was all just a big mistake. I must have been out of my mind. What kind of girl spends all her time with a guy whose ego is that humongous?" She stared straight at Skyler.

Careful. This is no time to get clever.

But Skyler didn't seem to catch the subtle barb. After all, egomaniacs of Skyler's proportions were never aware that they were egomaniacs.

"You know what?" she said. "I want to write Jake an e-mail. I do. I want to give him a piece of my mind. I mean, high school's over anyway, right? What high school relationship has ever made it past the first two weeks of college? I should just give him one big fat official kiss-off. A last goodbye. You know?"

Skyler perked right up at the notion—even more than Gaia had expected. "A last goodbye. . . ," he mused. "*Yes.* I think that's a brilliant idea. He deserves it. A nice little well-written 'Dear Jake' e-mail. Oh, you've got to do it."

You'd just love that, wouldn't you, Skyler? You'd love to see me clear the decks of anyone who stands between you and sole ownership of Gaia Moore. You make me sick.

"Can I use your laptop?" she asked.

"Absolutely." He grinned. "Hell, I'll help you write it."

Of course you will. Aren't you just oozing with generosity?

Skyler grabbed Gaia's hands and lifted her off the couch, pulling her across the room to his laptop and placing her in his desk chair, hovering behind her as he massaged her shoulders.

With her back to him, Gaia took this rare opportunity to actually wince at his touch. She'd been holding in all the winces for so long, she had to at least let one of them go. Then she pulled his laptop closer.

Here it was, sitting right in her hands. The only other potential source of evidence in this apartment. Skyler had surely deleted anything incriminating from his hard drive. But that still left his e-mail. There was still a chance that she could nab something legit from an e-mail folder. There was just one little problem. . . . She would need his password.

Gaia went online to get web access to her e-mail. She quickly typed in her user name, and then she entered her password.

The absolutely wrong password.

The expected message popped up in red. *Invalid entry. Please reenter your password.*

"Whoops," Gaia muttered. She typed in the very wrong password again and waited for the message again. "What the hell?" she groaned. She typed in the wrong password again and again until she finally got a message suggesting that she contact her e-mail server to correct the problem. *Perfect.* She smacked her hand down on the desk with gusto. "Goddammit! Stupid computers. I *hate* these things."

Then she leaned back slowly, rubbing her head up and down against Skyler's flat stomach, staring up at him with that doe-eyed girlie-girl expression she'd been practicing all day. "My e-mail sucks," she pouted. "Can we use yours?" she asked helplessly.

Skyler laughed and gave her a condescending pat on the head. "Sure," he said.

Such a gentleman. Such a stupid *gentleman.*

Gaia stood up from the chair and let Skyler sit down to sign in to his e-mail. She could tell he was hesitating to enter his password with her standing so close, so she immediately stepped away and turned for the kitchen. "I'm going to need a drink for this," she joked.

She took a few more steps toward the kitchen until Skyler felt secure in typing his password, and then she whipped her head back over her shoulder and focused in on the keyboard. Here was yet another thing Skyler didn't know about her. Her vision was far beyond average. She could pinpoint the smallest of moving targets from fifty to a hundred yards away. Which made this child's play. Her eyes darted along the keyboard, following his fingers as he typed each letter.

S-k-y-M-a-s-t-er-1-6.

Bingo. Thank you, Skyler. That was all I needed.

She turned back for the kitchen and grabbed a soda from the fridge. *SkyMaster16. . .* How disgustingly appropriate. One simple password spoke volumes about his conceited ass. He really did see himself that way. As a "master." Or more to the point, as *her* master. Once again Gaia had to clamp down on her temper. Because it was all so hopelessly familiar. It was shades of Oliver all over again. She'd seen enough of Oliver's top secret memos in the past year—memos referring to her as the "subject." It was her least favorite word in the world. And it had to stop. Gaia had to prove it once and for all: She was nobody's subject. And no one was her master.

"Okay," Skyler said excitedly, giving up his chair to Gaia. "We're good to go."

"You're so sweet to help me with this," she said, squeezing his arm in just the right place. "What would I do without you?"

"Nothing, I hope." He smiled.

Gaia pulled the laptop closer and they began to work on her "Dear Jake" e-mail. She could explain the whole ridiculous scenario to Jake later, once this whole thing was over. Which Gaia hoped would be very soon.

From: SJRodke@rodke.ind.com
To: jakem@alloymail.com
Time: 8:37 PM
Re: Last goodbye

Dear Jake,

Don't be confused by the e-mail address. I'm writing to you from Skyler's house, which I actually think is pretty appropriate. Maybe you'll finally accept where my loyalties are.

That last phone call really pissed me off, Jake. I was trying to be polite and have an amicable conversation with you about this whole prom situation, but you had to turn it into another stupid fight, which is pretty much all we seem to do now. Fight.

I know your oversized ego probably won't be able to deal with this, but I'm writing to you to make it official. Whatever we had. . . it's over.

Let's face it, Jake. School is ending, and I think that we should end with it. You'll be going off to college, and I'm not even sure what I'm going to do next, but whatever it is, we never would have lasted long distance. Our lives are just headed in completely different directions.

I hope in the future you can grow up a little and learn how to control your ego. Because it's just going to keep getting you into trouble, Jake. And leave you feeling very much alone.

Let's try not to complicate this too much. You don't need to write back. Let's just try to end it gracefully and go our separate ways, all right? Don't write back with some angry e-mail and drag this out any further.

So this will be our last goodbye, Jake.

I hope you have a nice life.

Best,

                            Gaia

JAKE CHECKED HIS WATCH. NINE P.M.
on the dot and not a soul in sight.

He stood alone in the center of **Eat Me**
the vacant lot on West Twelfth Street,
spinning slowly in place, checking
and rechecking every dark corner, waiting for Chris
Rodke. But there was nothing. Just two half-shattered
streetlights casting dim, ugly light on the broken gray
asphalt.

There wasn't an ounce of wind blowing, which
made for an eerie stillness. It was a bit like
standing on the surface of the moon, looking out into nothing but a vacuum of black space.
There wasn't a star in the polluted sky. The only sound
was the distant din of the cars down on the highway,
more and more of them approaching and then
whizzing by without a sign of Chris.

Jake could literally feel each minute ticking by far
too slowly, and it was starting to get to him. It was
making him antsy. Nervous, even. He began to walk,
listening to the sound of his footsteps scraping across
the garbage and the broken glass on the ground. But
he could walk only so far in any direction. Every corner tapered off into a pitch-black alley or the cold
brick wall of a meat-packing warehouse. It left him no
choice but to turn himself around and walk the length
of the lot again and again, crisscrossing the
empty space like a rat in a cage.

He'd spent the entire day trying to convince himself that Chris wouldn't stand him up. But after ten minutes of pacing the abandoned lot, his heart began to sink.

That lying son of a bitch. This supposed meeting was just another joke to him. Another humiliating slap in Jake's face.

After fifteen minutes had passed, Jake shoved his hands in his pockets and tried to accept it. Chris wasn't going to show. It was time to give up and move on. He dropped his head and began a slow, plodding walk back toward the street.

And then he heard it. The whispering of his name.

He stopped in his tracks and whirled around to trace the origin of the whisper.

"*Jake,*" the voice whispered again. It was coming from the pitch-black alley, just around the corner of the warehouse.

"Chris?" Jake stared at the dark alley. "You're late, asshole."

There was no response.

Jake was getting pissed. "What are you *hiding* from, Chris? It's just me. I'm alone."

Still no response.

"Jesus, what is your problem?" Jake barked. He moved toward the alley. "Just come out where I can see you."

"Eat me," the voice whispered.

"Excuse me? Come *out* of there, you freaking coward."

"*Eat* me, asshole," the voice replied. Now Jake could hear him laughing. *Laughing.*

Jake's fists clenched up like rocks. He stomped toward the dark black hole. If he had to drag Chris out into the light, that was more than fine with him. He stepped into the darkness and reached for any part of Chris's body he could get his hands on.

And then Jake howled. From the pain. The excruciating pain. . .

His hand. A bat. . . or a lead pipe. . . crushing his hand against the wall. The sound of his own guttural scream echoed off the brick walls of the narrow alley. Jake fell to his knees, cradling his shattered hand against his chest. But the rock-hard heel of a boot kicked his head back, knocking him to the ground, where the shattered glass sliced into the back of his neck. Jake screamed again from the pain.

And then they were everywhere. Pouring out of the alley like cockroaches. Jake's eyes were spinning dizzily out of control from the kick. The Droogs were swirling in and out of his crooked field of vision. Shaved heads and shirtless wiry torsos. Maniacal grins and black dilated pupils. Bats and pipes and broken bottles were suddenly raining down on every inch of his body. Relentless kicks to his chest and head.

Jake's brain was only half functioning. *Trap*, he hollered at himself. *Setup. Ambush.*

But the screams in his own head were being drowned out by the gleeful giggles pouring from the mouths of the Droogs.

"Eat me," they chanted between howls and giggles. If they weren't whaling on him, then they were aimlessly smashing their pipes against the ground, bouncing up and down like a pack of wild animals who'd just escaped the zoo. *"Eat me, Jake! Eat me!"*

They were collapsing in a huddle over him, ugly faces darting in and out from overhead. There was no chance to think, no chance to move. Just blow after agonizing blow. An overload of exquisite pain.

But finally one last thought made it through to Jake's consciousness. One primal thought fueled by rage and adrenaline...

Fight. Get off the ground and rip these lunatics apart.

Jake dug down and found a well of untapped energy. He rolled to his side and swept the legs of three of them, sending them toppling to the ground. Then he focused all his power on his back, shooting himself up off the ground and landing squarely on both feet. He whipped around and snapped himself into a state of pure focus. Adrenaline had momentarily stripped his entire body of pain. And he needed to use that moment for all it was worth. He put his hands forward in a combat stance and reminded himself that the Droogs weren't even animals. They were all just insects—cockroaches. Aimless and mindless and easily crushed.

A pipe came swinging for his head, but he ducked under it, grabbing the pipe in one hand and the psycho's arm in the other. He twisted his attacker's arm right out of its socket and hurled him over his head, smacking his wiry frame against the wall.

Two more came at him with knives, but he threw his elbow deep into one of their stomachs—cracking his ribs—and then spun into a roundhouse kick that connected with the other's face, knocking him into two more Droogs as they collapsed in a confused heap.

And then he went on the attack. He twirled the pipe in his hand, distracting one of their feeble minds just before he jabbed it into the guy's gut. Then he grabbed one of the skinny bastards' necks and smashed his face straight into the wall.

But with each one that went down, two more seemed to pile on—louder and less daunted than the last. Their bloodstreams were coursing with Invince. They felt no pain, no fear. And there were so many. . . .

Jake took another three of them down with a swift combination. He smashed the pipe against two of their faces and smacked two more faces with a high-flying kick and a swift elbow. But he could feel reality creeping up on him. His one adrenalized moment was passing and he knew it. He could feel the pain again, dismantling his hand—wrecking his coordination.

And then they all drove at him en masse—a `swift, powerful blitz` that flattened him up against the wall. They all began pummeling his body with kicks and bashes until they'd driven him back down to the ground.

There were too many of them. Too many to see. Too many to fight. . .

Their howls and chants echoed off the walls of the empty lot.

"God hates you, asshole! God hates you, asshole!"

Their voices started to meld into a hellish chorus of deafening noise. Jake could no longer see, and he could hardly hear. Lying there semiconscious, kicked in the head again and again, he could only make out the last few words. . . .

"God says goodbye. . . ."

I've been sitting in the same chair for about an hour, trying to figure out why I agreed to take Heather Gannis to her prom when I've barely even talked to the girl for months and months. I admit it's kind of an odd decision. After all, things didn't exactly end well between us. Or rather, I should say, our breakup was a total disaster. A ten-car pileup, soap-opera-from-hell kind of disaster. A disaster that left the odds of us ending up as prom dates somewhere in the "hell-freezing-over" category.

But then again, I've pretty much given up on the concept of odds and probability. Once you've died and come back to life, you kind of stop asking yourself questions like, "What are the odds?"

But maybe that's the point.

I mean, I went ahead and considered every possible reason I could think of for saying yes to Heather.

1. Maybe deep down, I felt I owed

her something after dumping her for
Gaia in the worst possible way.

But I don't think it's that.

2. Maybe it's really just a
subconscious excuse to see Gaia
again, even though we've drifted
almost completely apart. (I'd put
the odds on her even going to her
prom at about 50-50. . . . Oh,
right. I don't do that anymore.)

But I don't really think it's
that either.

I think maybe what it really
comes down to *is* probability.
Because Heather and I have both
beaten the odds.

The thing that ultimately
binds us is that we're both sur-
vivors. We went through the fire,
and somehow we've come out on the
other side. *Alive.* And I have to
say, there's something extremely
compelling about the idea of
spending one truly normal evening
with Heather Gannis again—just as
a shining symbol to us both that
we've made it back. We made it
back to the real world—where an
organic chemistry final *is* the

main thing to worry about, where true bravery can be an act as simple as calling up your old boyfriend whom you haven't spoken to forever and asking him to your senior prom.

And Heather wasn't just brave, she was. . . humble. There was just a certain sweetness that I hadn't heard in Heather's voice since. . . well. . . ever. Heather Gannis. . . humble and sweet. What were the odds?

I'm not blaming the pain Heather and I went through on Gaia. I mean, all the decisions in my life were my own. I take full responsibility. And you can't say that Gaia didn't warn me. She did. She warned me time and time again not to get too close to her life. And as much as I'll always care for the girl and as much as I would climb out of this chair right now and risk my life for her again, I must finally admit that she was right. . . .

Getting close to Gaia Moore can be dangerous.

He slid his
hand over her
collarbone and
grabbed the
back of her
neck, pulling
her
closer,
bringing their
lips too close,
too fast.

chop
the
monkey

THE REPORTS WERE FLOODING OLIVER'S
earpiece faster than he could handle.

Rabid Dogs

"Sir, there are at least twenty of them, maybe thirty," the voice crackled in his ear.

"Sir, we need to move in *now*, sir!" another voice shouted, nearly blowing out the receiver.

Oliver's binoculars nearly fell from his hands at the sight of it. He had never seen such chaos in all his years as an agent. So many of them pouring out of the dark alley like demons. All of them as mad as savages, fixated on one mission and one mission only: to murder Jake Montone.

"*Move in!*" he hollered, dropping the binoculars to the floor of his car. "*Move!*"

He kicked open the car door and raced across the dark empty street, listening to the sound of his own heavy breaths as he searched for a sign of Jake amid the flailing bodies and brutal blows.

His army of gray-suited agents stormed the lot with their guns cocked and ready. They fired rounds of warning shots into the air, but that seemed to have no effect. These demons were so deranged that nothing seemed to faze them. No amount of gunshots or commands seemed to sway them from their singular mission. They just kept on giggling—howling and scratching at Jake's body like a pack of rabid dogs.

"Take them down!" Oliver ordered. "Go for the legs!"

His agents started firing into the ground, puncturing the savages' legs as blood splattered across the gray asphalt. Some of the boys finally began to fall.

Oliver grabbed onto one of their backs and jabbed his knee deep into his spine, throwing him aside. He grabbed another by the neck and hurled him over his back, sending his writhing body crashing against the brick wall. His agents followed suit, laying into the boys with swift, incapacitating blows—a kick to the windpipe, blinding punches to the face. There was so much blood building up in puddles on the ground. But Oliver's eyes stayed fixed on his target.

Jake. He had to plow through the pack and get to Jake.

After stabbing his elbow into the back of one of their necks and bashing one of their heads with the barrel of his gun, he finally saw Jake's body. Unmoving. Bruised and bleeding and limp.

But still conscious. Thank God, still conscious.

Oliver fired two bullets into one of their legs, sending him to the ground, and then he grabbed Jake's shoulders, dragging him from the fray and propping him up against the wall.

"Jake!" he shouted. "Jake, can you hear me?"

"Okay. . . ," Jake mumbled through his swollen lips. "I'm okay. . . ."

Oliver's agents were finally managing to contain the savages. Many of them were strewn out across the blood-soaked pavement, dragging themselves along the ground with their hands—still laughing gleefully, uttering nonsensical ramblings.

"God says eat me." They laughed. "God says good-bye. . . ."

A few of them finally scurried off back down the alley in retreat. Their giggles were echoing off the enclosed walls, floating up high overhead.

But it was over. The carnage was over.

"That son of a *bitch*," Oliver muttered, pulling a handkerchief from his pocket and wiping the blood from Jake's face. "I *knew* it. I knew it was a trap, and I let you walk right into it. I should have known better."

Oliver's entire crew had been staked out in positions all over the perimeter of the lot for this very reason: the likelihood of a possible ambush. But still. . . it had taken them too long. Oliver had gotten there too late. They should have been on the scene in less than five seconds, not thirty. Jake shouldn't have had a bruise on him. Oliver never should have even let Jake walk into this trap in the first place.

"I'm sorry," Oliver breathed with a noxious combination of anger and guilt.

"Not your fault. . . ," Jake uttered, pushing his hands down on the ground to pick himself back up. "We didn't have a choice," he grumbled, using all his effort to rise. But he was still too weak. His first two attempts failed.

"Don't move," Oliver insisted. "Just be still, Jake. Be still."

He checked Jake's body, trying to assess the severity of his cuts and bruises. And then he felt a sudden hitch in his heart. Some inexplicable swelling of emotion in his chest. For Jake. It was a feeling Oliver couldn't decipher. Some bizarre mix of failure and loss and responsibility. The deeper he searched his feelings, the more he could only liken it to certain feelings he'd had for Gaia.

Paternal feelings. That's what these were. He felt like a father trying to tend to his child's wounds—trying to overcome his guilt for somehow failing him, for not being there when he needed him the most. After all those arguments in the loft—all that insistence that Oliver was anything but Jake's father, there were apparently some very real feelings to the contrary.

But Oliver blocked them out. He regained his senses and shook off the foolish burst of emotion.

This is ridiculous, he shouted at himself. *Jake is no son to you, he's just a pawn. That is all. He is nothing more than a necessary pawn in your quest to regain Gaia's loyalty—to bring her back into the fold, alive and unharmed. Stop acting like such a fool.*

"Sir, this is KS5 reporting, sir." The voice of Oliver's operative piped in through the earpiece still buried in his ear. "We have a development on the perimeter."

Oliver pressed his hand against his earpiece and spoke up. "Come back? I didn't catch that."

"Repeat, we have a development on the perimeter of the scene, sir. We've got military presence. I repeat, we've got military presence on the scene. Two soldiers in fatigues, sir—I'd say PFCs. They are currently staked out in a military vehicle approximately twenty yards from the lot. Binoculars, sir—both of them are observing the scene."

Oliver's brow furrowed with deep confusion. *Military?* What the hell was military doing there? What interest could they possibly have in this `nightmare` on `Twelfth Street`? He was going to find out, that was for goddamn sure.

"Monitor their actions," he ordered. "Do you copy? We are contained down here. I want you observing those men. I want *everything*. I want visual surveillance, I want audio surveillance. Monitor every communication they make, everything. Do you copy?"

"Copy that sir," his operative replied. "Surveillance is under way."

"What's going on?" Jake croaked, staring at Oliver's confused expression.

"I don't know yet," he said, trying to think it through. "But I'm going to find out. Can you stand?"

"Yeah." Jake's breathing was still labored.

"You're sure?"

"*Yes*," he insisted. Jake clenched his teeth, fighting

off the pain, and he climbed back to his feet slowly, stumbling to stay upright. Oliver threw Jake's arm around his shoulders and began walking him back gingerly toward the car.

"I'm sorry," Jake said, pushing Oliver away and forcing himself to walk unassisted.

"For what? I never should have let you walk into that trap."

"I could have *taken* those assholes," Jake said. He stumbled again and Oliver quickly propped him back up, keeping his arm wrapped around his shoulders. "If I'd known what was coming, I could have taken every one of them."

"Don't be ridiculous," Oliver said. "There were too many of them. You did everything you could. You impressed the hell out of me."

"I did?" Jake turned to him.

"You did," Oliver said. "You reminded me of someone," he uttered under his breath. He hadn't meant to say it out loud.

"Who?"

"What?"

"Who did I remind you of?"

"Forget it," Oliver said. "He was a Green Beret. A fighter. Brilliant with hand-to-hand combat. You reminded me of him."

"But who was he?"

"Never *mind* that," Oliver snapped, carefully helping

Jake into his car. Oliver didn't want to think about that man. It was the last thing he wanted to think about right now—the pathetic sob story of a young fool named Oliver Moore—who had never had a child of his own. And never would.

"Our only focus is Chris Rodke," Oliver said coldly. "He's all we need to talk about right now—he's all we need to think about. And when I get my hands on that little bastard and I get all the information I need. . . I will not be held accountable for the actions that follow."

Memo

From: KS5
To: L

Monitored all aspects of military presence as
ordered. Witnessed the following:

The soldiers completed their observation of
the incident and then placed a call to a "General
Colter." Below is the soldier's cell phone conversation (recorded and noted):

Soldier: General Colter? Yes, sir. We
have witnessed the incident, sir. There were
injuries, no casualties. But it was an ugly
scene, General. There was a rescue of the
victim by an unidentified party, but the evidence is sufficient. The Rodke boy was not
lying to you, sir. This drug is bad news.
Extremely ugly, sir. They were like animals
on the stuff. Deranged. Subhuman, I would
say, sir. They would have decimated their
victim, and then I think they would have decimated each other. I'm a Christian man, and
this was some unholy stuff, sir. [Pause] Yes,
sir. Reporting back to base now.

That was the end of the communication. The
soldiers pulled out of position and drove north.
Please advise.

Memo

From: L
To: KS5

This is excellent work. You have more than
made up for your prior failures. If my instincts
are correct, then this is the pivotal piece of
information I was missing. I believe the boy may
be within our reach. Await further instructions.
And send medical supplies to the loft ASAP.

DR. RODKE WAS NOT ONE TO PANIC.

Phase Two

He kept a stiff upper lip. He never let anything faze him. It was one of the keys to his success. But after hearing General Colter's voice on the phone, he couldn't help it. He was panicked. Something was wrong. He could hear it in the general's voice. Colter was pissed, and Rodke was now sweating bullets under his Brooks Brothers jacket. His blood pressure was rising. Even his driving was erratic. He'd already run two red lights in his Mercedes, and he'd nearly sideswiped a taxi, pounding angrily on his horn like the most low-class of New Yorkers. It was downright embarrassing to be so frazzled.

The general had demanded an immediate meeting, but he wouldn't say why. All he'd said was for Rodke to meet him on the corner of Rector Street and Broadway and to be there within fifteen minutes. Rodke had barely used his brakes for the entire drive downtown. He'd prayed the whole way that he wouldn't have any run-ins with the NYPD.

What could have gone wrong? It had to be about that missing contract. Rodke was sure Chris had stolen it, and he'd had his people out searching for Chris all day with no luck. But what could Chris have possibly done with that classified information? What could a seventeen-year-old boy possibly do to screw up this deal? Rodke couldn't think of a thing, and that

117

was what was panicking him the most. Not knowing.

He finally made it down to Rector Street, and he could see the general's limo parked on the corner. Rodke pulled up right behind the general and got out of his car. He activated the alarm and then trotted toward the limo as the back door swung open, a signal for him to get in. He leaned down and peered into the car's dimly lit interior. A lone shaft of light illuminated the general's icy expression. He was sitting on the black leather seat, alone and impatient.

"Get in," Colter ordered.

Rodke had never been one to take orders, but in this case he had to make an exception. He gathered himself and climbed into the seat opposite the general.

"All right, what's the problem?" Rodke demanded.

"Close the door," Colter ordered.

Rodke was so frazzled, he hadn't even remembered the door. He leaned forward and slammed it closed, sitting back in his seat and staring expectantly at Colter in the near darkness. "So. . . ?"

Colter fixed his cold stare on Rodke. It was a punishing stare. A "shame-on-you" stare. The kind of look Rodke had given Chris a thousand times before. It was offensive as hell.

"The deal is off," Colter declared.

"What are you talking about?" Rodke forced a half smile, as if the general were possibly joking. "We've already signed the contracts."

"That contract is null and void."

"Null and void?" He let out another puff of nervous laughter. "I don't see what could possibly—"

"You're a liar, Rodke."

"*Excuse* me?"

"You heard what I said. That contract is a bunch of lies. One *hundred* percent free of side effects? One *hundred* percent safe? That's the biggest load of crap I've ever heard. That stuff is a goddamn nightmare. That stuff turns men into animals. You wanted to put *my* soldiers on that stuff? What kind of sicko are you?"

"I'm sorry, I—I—" Rodke was stammering with confusion. Where the hell was all this coming from? "General, we haven't even completed the prototype for the drug. How could you possibly—?"

"Your son Chris was kind enough to set up a little demonstration for me. He showed me what that drug does to people. He opened my eyes, and thank God he did, Rodke. That's all I can say for you. Thank God he did."

Chris. I knew it.

Rodke was suddenly so livid, he could hardly breathe. He'd been blindsided by his own son. Chris had gotten to the general somehow. And he'd obviously set up some sort of dog-and-pony show using his drug-addict test subjects for his "demonstration." That petty, vengeful little. . . Chris had finally taken his jealousy and his resentment too far. He was using Invince to try to blow the deal when he didn't even know the real details of the operation. For a moment Rodke honestly felt like strangling his own son. But he couldn't let his anger get the better of him. He would deal with Chris later. Right now he needed to do some serious and immediate damage control.

He would have to let Colter in on *all* the details of the operation. He simply had no choice if he wanted to save this deal.

"All, right, General, just hold on," Rodke insisted. "Just relax for a moment and listen to me, all right? My *son* is the one giving you the misinformation, and I can explain."

"What can you explain? This drug turns men into savages. Explain *that*."

"Look, I'm sure that whatever you saw was very ugly, but you need to understand this, General. . . The drug that those lunatics were on—Invince—that is *not* the drug we are selling you. The drug that Chris has been distributing is a very *old,* very *early* test version of the pill."

"An old version. That's your excuse?"

"It's no excuse. It's the truth. Invince was an early prototype that was *accidentally* leaked to the public by my son." It was, in fact, no accident, but Colter didn't need to know that right now.

"Well, where the hell's the *new* version of the drug?" Colter snapped. "Get to the goddamn point, Rodke."

"I am getting to the point, General, if you would just listen. The point is, my people are just now in the process of developing the *final* prototype for the drug. The perfect version of the drug. The version that we will be selling to you."

"Well, what the hell's the holdup? And give it to me in English. I don't want to hear a bunch of scientific mumbo jumbo."

"That is what I'm trying to do, General. I will give it to you in plain English." He took a breath to stay calm and composed. "Okay, here's the thing about this pill," Rodke began. "You have to understand, the fearless properties of this pill are all derived from this one. . . specimen—this one. . . animal. She is a *very rare* animal that for some reason is genetically immune to fear."

"What kind of animal?"

"What kind of animal. . . ?"

"Yes. What kind of animal is this *'she'*? I obviously need to know a hell of a lot more than you're telling me."

Apparently a few white lies would be necessary. "Well. . . she's a primate."

"A monkey."

"Yes, that's right," Rodke lied. "She's a monkey. And we have been using her DNA samples—this. . . monkey—to create our early prototypes for the drug. We wanted to run as many tests as possible using a *live* specimen. But that was only phase one of our study,

121

General. We've always known that a live specimen would only provide us with so much information. But we are now in the final stages of the operation, and we've been prepping her for phase two."

"And what is *phase two?*" The general looked dubious.

"Well. . . phase two will be the complete dissection of the specimen."

Colter stared long and hard at Rodke. "So you're telling me you need to chop up this monkey to get all the info you need? That's it? That's the holdup?"

Rodke coughed with discomfort. When the general put it that way, it made him feel a little ill. Perhaps even a little guilty about what they were doing to her. But he recovered quickly. "Well. . . yes. That is basically what I'm telling you. The DNA samples alone were never going to give us all the information we needed. The biology behind her fearlessness is extremely complicated, and it needs to be studied in total. In order to create the perfect prototype for the drug, Dr. Ulrich needs to dissect the specimen. He needs to do a full autopsy on her—examine every one of her organs individually—the heart, the brain, the spine, etc. Then we'll have the final results we need, and then we can build you the perfect drug. I-25d. The final prototype. No side effects, as promised. One hundred percent effective and one hundred percent safe."

Colter sat there in silence, processing the information and sizing up Rodke with a long, discomforting stare. "This better not be a bunch of bull," he said finally.

"This is no bull, General, I assure you."

Another painful silence.

"All right, fine," Colter huffed. "I'll give you seventy-two hours. That's it. You tell your people to chop up that goddamn monkey ASAP. You chop her into as many pieces as you need, and you get me a drug that works. Otherwise the deal is off."

"Absolutely," Rodke said, holding back his slight nausea at Colter's choice of words. "I've got my people working on it right now. The autopsy will be done by tomorrow night."

"It better be. Now get out."

Colter swung open the door and didn't give Rodke another look.

"We'll be speaking shortly," Rodke said pointlessly.

He got out of the limo and walked back to his car, picking up the pace with every step.

Chris, you're going to have to pay for this. Somehow, some way, you are going to have to pay.

Rodke's pulse began to quicken again with nerves. Everything had to be rushed now, and he hated that. But there was no longer any choice in the matter, thanks to Chris. He had to get in touch with Skyler and let him know. They were bumping up the schedule and they were moving to phase two as of right now. He had to meet with Ulrich ASAP to shore up the plan. They needed to start prepping the lab posthaste. No ifs, ands, or buts. . .

Her autopsy needed to be over and done with by tomorrow night.

"SO, GAIA, I'VE BEEN THINKING.

About this whole prom thing. . ."

Skyler poured them each a glass of red wine

Manhandled

and then he sat back down on the couch, lifting Gaia's legs onto his lap and pulling her closer. Gaia couldn't stand to be manhandled, but she grinned playfully. "What about it?" she asked.

"Well. . ." He took a sip of wine and swished it around in his mouth like a connoisseur. What a pretentious ass. She smiled again. "I gotta be honest here. . . ."

"Oh, by all means," Gaia said, sipping from her wine. "I want us to be completely honest with each other, Skyler." Had more absurd words ever been spoken?

"Well, I've just been thinking about our talk before and about the e-mail to Jake, and I've got to tell you, I really don't think we should go to this prom."

"You don't?"

"I honestly don't. I mean, let's look at the facts. We've already established that you never really made any friends at this school. There's really no one you'd want to see there."

Well, almost no one. But the people she'd want to see probably wouldn't want to see her at this point.

"And I really don't think you want to be sitting there in that hideously decorated Supper Club, surrounded by a bunch of kids in poufy dresses who think that the senior prom is the be-all, end-all of existence. That's just not you."

She had to give it to him. He was right about that, too.

"And I know why," he said. "There is a very obvious reason that you just don't fit in with those kids."

Now this she wanted to hear. Gaia would even accept insights from her archnemesis on this topic. If someone honestly thought they knew why she lived in a permanent state of alienation, she was all ears. "Why?" she asked, sounding more curious than she'd intended.

"Because," Skyler said. He leaned closer and examined every aspect of her face, landing squarely on her eyes. "You're just not a kid. It's that simple. You're a woman living in a seventeen-year-old's body. That's why you never fit in. That's why you can't make these 'kid' relationships work with these *boys*. It's everything about you. . . the way you talk, the way you think. I mean, it's in your eyes. These inhuman blue eyes of yours. . . even your eyes are speckled with gray. There's all this wisdom in them—like you've seen everything already—distant lands and epic battles." He laughed. "Like you're Odysseus or something, you know? Just. . . an incredibly beautiful female version. . ."

Skyler trailed off, but his eyes stayed locked with hers. And God help her, she couldn't break the eye contact. Not because she was playing her flirtation game, but because Skyler had managed to strike at something again. Something real. Something painfully true about her fish-out-of-water existence.

He was right. She wasn't a kid. She didn't even know how to be one. And she'd already lost her chance. She'd ceased to be a kid the night her father had abandoned her in that hospital at the age of twelve, while she was still reeling with shock from the death of her mother.

Maybe she was never really a kid. As far as she could tell, so much of growing up seemed to be learning how to overcome your fears, but her fears had been overcome since the day she was born—with the exception of a few very insane weeks of her life. Maybe that was why she was so unbearably cynical. Because she had basically been an adult for seventeen years. And she had been completely sapped of optimism.

She probably would have stayed pathetically glued to

126

Skyler's eyes for minutes more had it not been for the gunfire.

A sudden thunderous blast of machine-gun fire flooded the room, nearly puncturing Gaia's eardrums and shaking the floor. The sound of shattering windows was deafening. Skyler's entire body shook as his glass of wine went crashing to the ground.

But Gaia didn't even flinch. Her glass stayed perfectly still in her hand.

Because it was just the TV. The TV had suddenly turned itself on for some reason, and some crappy action movie was on HBO, with the volume turned up far too loud.

"*Jesus.*" Skyler belted out a loud, nervous laugh of relief. His shoulders were still hunched up from the shock of the noise. He grabbed the remote and flipped off the TV, and then he slapped his hand over his head. "Oh God, it was the *timer,*" he groaned. "I set the TV timer for nine-thirty this morning, but I must have pressed p.m. by mistake." He took another breath and laughed, turning back to Gaia. "*God,* that scared me." But as he stared at Gaia and her perfectly intact glass of wine, his giggle died off. And then a curious look came over his face. Gaia couldn't understand what the odd look in his eyes meant.

But then it hit her. It hit her like a ton of proverbial bricks.

You forgot to be scared, you idiot! You were so caught up in your little self-pitying moment, you forgot to look

*like a startled little waif for Skyler. Do something. Do
something now.*

"Oh. . . my. . . God. . ." She brought her hand slowly
over her heart. "Look at me. I am literally petrified." She
blew out a long breath of fake relief. "I
swear to God, I thought it was the beginning of World
War *Three*." She shook out her hand as if she were trying to shake off the fear. "Oh, *no*," she moaned in her
best mommy voice. She put her wine down on the coffee table. "Come here, you poor thing. You dropped
your wine. Are you okay? *Damn* all that violence on
television," she joked.

"I'm okay," he giggled, sitting back against the
couch. "What about you?"

"Well, I'm fine *now*," she said, grasping his hands.
"That stupid TV timer," she whined. "That scared the
hell out of me."

"I'm really sorry," he said. "My bad. You're sure
you're all right. . . ?" There was still something not
right about the way he was looking at her. Some kind
of lingering suspicion. It was like he was
studying her face, searching for genuine signs of fear.
And that was a very bad sign. She had to stomp it out.
She had to distract the hell out of him immediately.

She quickly reached over and cradled his face in
her hand. "You know what. . . ?"

He raised an eyebrow. "What?"

"I just realized something."

"What's that?"

She leaned toward him. "You are monumentally cute." She examined his face from all sides. "You are. You are, like. . . movie-star cute." She didn't blink. She kept her eyes fixed on his. *Maintain eye contact. . . .*

"Oh, *nice.*" Skyler laughed. "You just realized that, did you?"

"What?" she squawked defensively. "Oh, come on, that's not what I meant."

"What did you mean?"

"Skyler. . . come on. . . you're, like, my brother or something. I mean. . . I'm not supposed to be attracted to my brother, right?"

Skyler's eyes widened. He seemed momentarily at a loss for words. She held her breath in the silence—partially to keep from feeling ill and partially praying that he was buying this.

"Um. . . that's true," Skyler said. "You're not supposed to be attracted to your brother. But I'm not." He leaned closer. "I'm not your brother."

"Hmmm. . . That's also true."

A suggestive little smile crept over his face. This was working. It was definitely working. "So does that mean I'm allowed to be attracted to you, too?" he asked quietly.

"Are you?"

He suddenly reached over and grabbed the collar of her T-shirt, pulling her dangerously close. "Now, that. . . is just a stupid question." He smiled. She could feel his warm breath against her lips as he spoke.

Okay, this was working much, much, much too well. Gaia broke out in a cold sweat. Not from fear, but from panic, pure and simple. She hadn't expected this. She hadn't expected him to move so fast. This was all talk. Just talk. But Skyler had forced her to back up the talk with action. And that was something else altogether.

She did not think she could do what it seemed like they were about to do. She did not *want* to do what it seemed like they were about to do. She did not want it with every ounce of her being. But she had done this to herself. She had upped the stakes on purpose. She couldn't pull back now. If she did, she'd only double his suspicion.

He slid his hand over her collarbone and grabbed the back of her neck, pulling her closer, bringing their lips too close, too fast. Too fast for her to stop it from happening.

But thank God almighty for that phone.

SKYLER'S CELL PHONE WENT OFF WITH a shrill electronic beep that snatched Gaia from the jaws of hell. He pulled away awkwardly and glanced down at the number.

Reptilian Film

Gaia pulled away fast and pushed herself back against the arm of the couch, breathing in the glorious distance between them and clenching her entire body under a thick, invisible shell.

"It's just a page," he mumbled. "Crap, I'm sorry, I have to deal with this for a minute—"

"That's okay," she assured him. It was beyond okay. Nothing could have possibly been more okay.

Skyler jumped up from the couch and walked across the room to his computer. "It'll just be a second," he called to her.

"Fine," she chirped.

He double-clicked a few times on the laptop. "Everything okay over there?"

"Fine," she replied, clamping her hands firmly between her knees.

"Have some more wine if you want."

"Okay."

She tried to mentally peel Skyler's reptilian film off her body.

Just breathe. You're cool now. Everything's cool. You've still got control of the situation. This is all under control.

"Oh, *man*," Skyler groaned.

She turned back to him. "What's wrong?"

"This dude," he complained. "This guy in my class. He's supposed to present for us tomorrow, but he doesn't have any of the notes. He's freaking out. He just sent me an e-mail—damn it." Skyler jumped up from his chair and tugged a notebook out of his bag. Then he trotted quickly across the room, grabbed his jacket, and threw it on. "I've got to go bring him these notes right now."

Gaia's antennae shot up. *E-mail.* Skyler had just gotten a page and an e-mail. From *them?* His father, Chris, Ulrich, whoever? It had to be, didn't it? Skyler had to be lying. Nobody ran out of the house in a panic just to bring some dude notes for a school presentation. That just didn't qualify as an emergency.

This was it. This was her shot. He was stepping out, probably to another one of their "top secret" meetings. And while they were out there discussing more of their demented plans, Gaia would just go ahead and raid that e-mail folder for some hard evidence.

Skyler ran over and knelt down next to her, leaning his elbows on the arm of the couch and shoving his face uncomfortably close to hers again.

"We'll just have to pick up where we left off when I get back." He grinned.

He was clearly giving Gaia a glimpse of Skyler Rodke's "bedroom eyes." It was a disgusting sight that she deeply wished she had not been forced to witness.

"Right," she breathed, forcing herself to smile.

She expected him to jump back up again, but he didn't. He stayed right where he was, tilting his head and gazing at her.

"What?" she asked, praying he wasn't waiting for a kiss goodbye. A real kiss.

"Here's what I think we should do," he announced. "*I* think. . . instead of wasting our time at the kiddie prom, we should just stay right here tomorrow night. And I will make you an unbelievable dinner. I'll get some very old wine from the Rodke stash, and we'll drink, and we'll eat, and I'll put on some music, and you and I will celebrate your official last night of being trapped in high school. Hell, we can even dance if you want," he added. "And then, when we've had enough to eat and enough to drink. . . we'll do whatever *else* we feel like doing. . . ." He flashed her another impish grin. There were those bedroom eyes again. Gaia did everything in her power not to puke right in his lecherous face. "It'll be a quiet romantic evening fit for two adults," he said. "No kids in poufy dresses allowed." He raised his eyebrows. "What do you think?"

What did she think? She thought it was abundantly clear that the Rodkes didn't want Gaia making any more public appearances.

"I think that sounds *perfect*."

"Good." He nodded proudly. "It's a done deal. You and me. Tomorrow night. In-house date. Two consenting adults," he joked. Not funny.

"*Yes,*" she agreed. "Absolutely."

"I gotta run. Will you be okay here for a while on your own?"

133

"As long as you're coming back," she said coyly.

"Well, I might be a while. Me and this guy. . . we might need to work on that presentation a little. If you're asleep when I get back, I promise not to be offended."

Gosh, how noble of you.

"Okay," she agreed. "I'll *miss* you, though. . . ."

"I'll miss you, too." He leaned forward but thankfully only went for the peck on the cheek. He stood up to leave, but then he seemed to have a follow-up thought. He dropped back down to his kneeling position. "Hey, let me ask you something."

"What?"

"I've just been thinking. . . . You know how in our e-mail to Jake, you were saying that you didn't even know what you'll do next? Once you're done with school?"

"Yeah?" Ugh. She had to remember to explain that e-mail to Jake ASAP.

"Well. . . what *do* you want to do next? I mean, have you decided on college yet?"

What with her busy schedule of defending her life, Gaia hadn't quite gotten around to college decisions just yet. She hadn't really gotten around to any thoughts about her future at all. Making it out of high school was about as much of a "goal" as she had set for herself. Making it out *alive,* that is. But her future never really felt secure enough to start planning what it would actually be like. A better question right now was, Why the hell did Skyler want to know?

"I guess I haven't quite thought that far ahead yet," she said. "Why?"

"Well, what if you could go anywhere?" he asked enthusiastically. "Like, the second you got that diploma in your hand, what if you could just disappear from all of this and go anywhere in the world? Where would it be?"

"You mean, like. . . with you?" she asked, beaming with false excitement. What was he after here? Was this part of their scheme? To whisk Gaia off to some exotic location or something? She would really like to see them try.

"*Maybe*," he said. "Seriously. What if it could be anywhere? What if we could just 'get lost' for a while? Your dream destination. Hawaii? Fiji. . . ?"

Gaia's mind split off in opposite directions. On the one hand, there was her growing suspicion about the Rodkes' "travel plans." But on the other, she couldn't help but consider the real answer to Skyler's question. What if she could just get lost? Where *would* she go once this was all over?

Her thoughts immediately turned to her brother. D was still out west on a farm in Ohio, trying to adjust to real life—life outside the walls of that horrific nightmare of an institution in Florida. That would be the first place she'd go. She would pack herself a bag and get on the first flight out to Ohio and she would visit D. Maybe she would stay with D and Daisy and her family for a bit. Breathe in some nonpolluted air for a change. Run her bare feet through some real green grass that hadn't been planted there by order of the mayor's office. Fall asleep to the sound of crickets instead of car alarms. Wake up to the smell of bales of hay instead of garbage and cigarette smoke wafting up from the street.

If she could *do* this. . . if she could take down the Rodkes—strike down the last round of enemies—put an *end* to the deadly psychodrama that she was still forced to refer to as her life—then D would be the first and only person she'd want to see. They could really talk for the first time. They could make some new memories that had absolutely nothing to do with Rainhill Hospital or Fort Myers Beach, Florida.

If she could make it out of this. It was all just one very big "if."

She turned back to Skyler. "Florida," she lied. "I just *love* Florida. I've had some of the greatest times of my life there."

Skyler looked delighted. "Florida, huh? Well, wouldn't you know it—Florida just happens to be one of my favorite places, too." He smiled.

"Oh, is that right?"

"Love it," he said. "Florida. . . *Very interesting. . .*" His grin grew wider. "I'll be back, okay? Don't wait up if I take too long." He gave her one last peck on the cheek, and then he skipped over to the door, shut it behind him, and locked it.

Gaia sat perfectly still for a five count, and then she leapt up from the couch and bolted across the room. She was sitting at his laptop by the count of ten. Now she was dying to know what this whole "traveling" scheme was about. Maybe the answer would be somewhere in his e-mail. Maybe all the answers she needed would be in his e-mail. She was praying for it.

She logged on, glancing back at the door and listening for any potential indication of his return. But he was definitely gone. She carefully typed in *SkyMaster16*, and at long last she was *in*. She pounded her index finger on the mouse and clicked on his in box. . . .

Damn it. Hardly anything was there. He had obviously deleted most of what he'd received. But he had yet to delete the last e-mail. The one he had just received. There was no subject, but there was an author. Oh, was there an author. *KTUlrich@rodke.ind.com*.

Ulrich. Yes. This was exactly what she was looking for. She was damn near salivating with excitement.

Until she opened the e-mail.

From: KTUlrich@rodke.ind.com
To: SJRodke@rodke.ind.com
Time: 9:44 PM
Re: No subject

Urgent change of plans. Chris has created
problems. We need to cut down our time frame con-
siderably. Your father has demanded a final prototype for the drug within 72 hours. This, of
course, means that we will be moving to phase two
immediately. You will need to complete your task
within 24 hours.

I will begin prepping the lab for a full
dissection and autopsy of the specimen. You
must report in for a strategy session ASAP.

—K.U.

I don't know how many times I reread the e-mail. No, not even the whole e-mail. I just kept rereading that one sentence.

I will begin prepping the lab for full dissection and autopsy of the specimen.

Dissection and autopsy. Of the *specimen*. As in *me*. Apparently I'm not even human enough to be a "subject" anymore. No, apparently I've been demoted to "specimen." I've been reduced to a frog in some sixth-grade science experiment, something you throw on a lab table and pin down so you can turn it inside out and look at all the parts. Please observe, fellow doctors: Here is Ms. Moore's fearless spleen. And here are her fearless kidneys. And here is Ms. Moore's fearless heart. As you can see, there is not much left of it.

Now it all makes sense. All of it. Every single dehumanizing step in their little plan.

That's why they gave me fear

in the first place. To pull me in
as their specimen. And to make me
vulnerable to Skyler. That's why
Skyler has been trying to keep me
stashed away in his apartment.
Not just to rip off more samples
of my DNA. That was only "phase
one." No, what they really wanted
was to prep me for phase two:
*dissection and autopsy of the
specimen.* They wanted to keep me
under strict supervision until it
was time to bump me off. To make
me disappear.

Assholes. A whole family of
sick, twisted assholes.

That's why Skyler was suddenly
talking to me about *travel plans.*
He's not planning our summer vacation to the Keys; he's planning my
"permanent vacation." A one-way
ticket to the great beyond. An
all-expenses-paid trip to Autopsy
City. It all just gets sicker.

Well, I've got news for the
Rodkes:

I have no intention of donating
my body to science anytime soon.
So if this is how they want to play

it, then this is how we'll play it.
I know what I need to know.
Somewhere in the next twenty-four
hours, they're going to try to take
me down and cut me up. And when they
do, I'll be waiting for it.

I've got to hand it to them.
They've done a brilliant job of
covering their tracks up until now.
But when they go for the kill,
that's when I'll catch them red-
handed. That's when I'll call in
the Agency. I'm not going to waste
my time trying to expose another
zillion-dollar drug company's dirty
dealings. They've got ten thousand
lawyers for that. They'll find a
bunch of loopholes and the Rodkes
will all get off scot-free. No, no,
no. I'm not going to let that happen. I'm ending this thing for
good. These assholes are going down
for attempted murder.

I'm watching for it, Skyler. I'm
waiting for you to make your move,
and my eyes are wide open. You're
the one who's in the dark now.
Because you don't see me coming.

From: Colter@mi.us.gov
To: CLRodke@rodke.ind.com
Time: 9:51 PM
Re: We need to meet

Christopher, this is General Colter. We have
witnessed the incident, and I am convinced that
you are not lying. This drug is bad news. We need
to meet. Same time, same place. Tomorrow night.
9:00 p.m. The lot on West Twelfth Street. Don't
be late.

From: CLRodke@rodke.ind.com
To: Colter@mi.us.gov
Time: 10:25 PM
Re: We need to meet

General. Glad to be of service. You have made
a wise decision. We have much to discuss. I will
see you at nine tomorrow.
    —Chris

Distant Memory

was. She was just thrilled to finally be getting some face time with Skyler. She'd been begging him for days to go to lunch, but he was, of course, his usual self—too busy, too many "social obligations," too much "on his plate." She had become used to her sweet brother's runaround tactics, and they generally didn't bother her, but in this case his avoidance had actually gotten on her nerves big time. There were just a few unanswered questions that were starting to drive Liz completely insane. So when Skyler had called her out of the blue for a late-night coffee, she'd been way more than happy to oblige. She'd hopped right into a cab and met him at Around the Clock immediately.

"So this is the best you can give me?" she joked. "Coffee at eleven at night? Nice. What a loving brother." She blew on her cereal-bowl-size latte.

"I know." Skyler sighed. "I'm a bad older brother. Guilty as charged. But at least you came out to meet me. I'm eternally grateful."

"Well, I forgive you this time," she said. "I'm sure there are worse brothers out there."

"Aw. You flatter me."

Liz gave him a playful slap on the arm just as he brought his black coffee to his lips. The coffee splattered

on his A/X T-shirt, and she felt that was sufficient punishment.

"Nice," he complained, dabbing his napkin in his
water and trying to wash it off. "Real nice." He
dropped the napkin and took a successful sip of his
coffee. "So, any luck with a prom date?"

Liz rolled her eyes. "You mean for this lousy school
I've attended for all of a month? I might as well be
attending the prom on Mars. But yes, I have procured the
necessary boy toy. James Wellington, of the Connecticut
Wellingtons." She rolled her eyes once more. "We've
played tennis twice in the Hamptons. Whatever. I'll just
be thrilled to have this high school nonsense over and
done with. How many high schools does this make in the
last four years? Three, I believe? Yes, thank you, Daddy,
for maintaining a Rodke headquarters in four different
cities."

"Well, at least we got to travel," Skyler said.

"Right. I just haven't seen enough of this great
country of ours. Whatever. I don't even understand
why he brought us to New York in the first place. Just
please get my ass to college. I want to know what it
feels like to be in the same place for four years. But
enough about me—*you* have some explaining to do,
speaking of prom dates." Liz flashed him the evil eye.

"What did *I* do?" Skyler laughed.

"What did you do? Hel-*lo*. I haven't heard from
Gaia in days. I was actually starting to worry about

her. Would you mind telling me what the *deal* is between you two? I mean, is she hanging out at your place or not? Are you two going to the prom, or is she going with Jake? I haven't seen Jake in a while either. What is going on? The girls at school keep asking me about her and I look like a complete ditz for not even knowing if she's hanging out with my own brother or not. Why am I completely kept out of the loop in this family?"

"Okay, okay." Skyler smiled. "My bad. Yes, Gaia has been hanging out with me, so you really don't need to worry about her. I'm sure she's sorry for not checking in with you, but you can blame me entirely. I guess some of my social flakiness has rubbed off on her."

"Mm-hmm," Liz muttered. "Well, what about the prom? Are you her date or not?"

"Ah, the prom," Skyler mused, gazing up toward the ceiling. Liz gave him another mini-slap on the arm. "Okay." He laughed. "Sorry. No, look, I'll tell you the truth. From what she's told me, I don't think Gaia could care less about the prom. She doesn't even want to go."

"What? You guys are going to leave me there all alone? That *sucks*. You're going to make me talk to James Wellington all night about backhands and serves?"

Skyler held up his hands in defense. "Hey, it wasn't my decision, sis. Honestly. . . I don't even know if I'm supposed to be telling you, but the way Gaia's been talking. . . I'm not even sure she's going to stick around for graduation."

"What?"

"I don't *know*," Skyler squawked. "I think she's just had it with the whole business. She's done. She's been telling me that she's thinking about just skipping town altogether."

"Uch, that's ridiculous. Doesn't she at least want to get the handshake and the diploma first? Why else do we endure four years of this high school nonsense? We do it for the handshake and the diploma."

Skyler shrugged. "Well, the way she's talking, I think she'd be more than happy to have the diploma mailed off to her. She says she's sick of this school, and she's pretty much sick of her life here in the city. She just wants to buy herself a one-way ticket to the Florida Keys and take a nice long vacation. I guess Florida's her favorite state or something. I tried to talk her out of it, *believe* me, but you know Gaia. She's so independent. Once she makes her mind up about something. . ."

Liz sighed with disappointment. "I think that's just really sad. I mean, not just for me at the prom, but for her, too. She made it this far; why is she going to run away now? That sucks."

"I know it." Skyler sighed. "But I guess she feels like she's worked too hard. She just wants to head down to the Keys for a nice long stretch of R & R. I can't really blame her."

"Well, is she even going to say goodbye to anybody? Me, Jake, *any*one?"

Skyler shook his head slowly. "Honestly? I don't even think she is going to say goodbye to anyone. I don't think anyone's going to hear from her for a long time. She just wants to forget high school altogether. And New York. She says she wants to lie out on some beach somewhere and just. . . 'get lost.' Whatever that means."

Liz sat there for a minute and stared at her coffee. This news made her even sadder than she would have expected. She really hadn't gotten the chance to know Gaia all that well, but she had honestly believed that they might have the chance to become truly good friends someday. Apparently she'd been wrong. Apparently Gaia was going to be like so many of the girls Liz had met along the way. She would just be another name that Liz couldn't quite remember from the past. Gaia Moore would end up as nothing more than a faint and distant memory.

It really was a shame.

Gaia was
stepping
down the
stairs,
ready for Ed **prom**
to escort **night**
her to the
prom.

From: megan21@alloymail.com
To: melanie@alloymail.com
Time: 6:16 PM
Re: Our night has arrived!

OMG, Mels! This is it, baby! I am so psyched! PROM NIGHT. Did you ever think we'd actually make it? Did you ever think we would finally cross that finish line?? Hallelujah!!!!!

Anyhoo, just checking in on all the deets. I confirmed the reservation for 10 of us. 8:00 at Balthazar. Mmm, moules frites. Rob is picking me up at 7:00, and the limo is starting with us at 7:15. We should get to you and Brad by 7:30. If din goes well, we should be at the Supper Club by 10:00. Fashionably late for a prom, yes? Yes.

I'm not ashamed to say it, btw. . . I look fabulous! The dress alterations were perfect, and I am totally trying your idea with the upsweep. I love it! You rule!

So let's go out there tonight and kick this school's ass with our collective bad selves!

GO, US!

See you soon,

Love,

Meegs

From: melanie@alloymail.com
To: megan21@alloymail.com
Time: 6:32 PM
Re: Our night has arrived!

Meegy! So glad about the hair idea. I could not
be more superpsyched for tonight. Brad should be
here by 7:15, so we'll be pressed and dressed to
the nines by 7:30 for the sweet, sweet limo! Thanks
for confirming the res, btw!

I must say, not to be too conceited, but as I
look in the mirror, I'm looking pretty damn fine
myself. I do believe that Tammie's vision is about
to become a reality.

We are gonna storm the Supper Club like queens!
There shall be no woman who can stealeth our thunder!
Lol. . . ☺

Seriously, though, I do believe that tonight it
shall be sealed in stone for all to remember. . .

We RULED this freakin SKEWL! And we will rule
this PRIZOM!

That is fo' shizzle, my sizzle!!

Ha ha. See you tonight, girl.

Love,

Mels

P.S. Can't wait to see Gaia in that black
potato-sack JC Penney funeral dress. Why is she
even going? Maybe we'll luck out and she'll be a
no-sho. More Jakein' for the takin'! Ha ha ha ☺

Purely Platonic

HEATHER HADN'T BEEN THIS NERVOUS in years. Quite possibly not since her first date, when she was thirteen years old and George Peltner took her to the 'N Sync concert. She had broken out in such a sweat that night that George had actually asked her if she'd gone swimming before the date. Of course, in the years that followed, she became something of a dating champion. The thought of being nervous for a date had become almost laughable for the great Heather Gannis. But tonight, as she waited for Sam Moon to ring her doorbell, she felt like she was starting all over again. Which, in many ways, she was.

She had grown accustomed to a certain amount of assisted living at the Carverton School for the Blind. Someone was usually there by her side, sometimes literally holding her hand to walk her through a difficult task. But this was her first night back home, and despite her family's incredible support—especially her mother's—she was feeling particularly *un*assisted right now. She was feeling very much on her own tonight, in this very blurry world. Maybe going to the prom wasn't such a good idea. The whole thing was feeling much more intimidating than she'd imagined it would be.

She couldn't even tell how she looked. She could see

the black outline of her strapless silk dress, and the white line that was the pearl necklace on her flesh, and the dark hair that framed her face. But for all she knew, the dress could be a disaster, the pearls could look prissy and stupid, and her hair could be a nightmare of split ends. Her mother insisted that none of these things were true, but Heather trusted no one's aesthetic opinion over her own, *especially* not that of her mother, who would say she looked beautiful if she were wearing a pink muumuu and a neon yellow golf visor.

She had actually come to love *not* caring about her appearance, and she felt almost ashamed for caring again tonight. Caring too much about appearances, after all, was a huge part of the old Heather that she didn't want to be anymore. But the fact was, tonight it mattered. It didn't have to matter any other night of the year, but tonight it just did, whether she liked it or not. She couldn't stop sweating. Her mother had given her a small black handkerchief so she could continuously dab the sweat that kept forming in tiny droplets all along her hairline.

When the doorbell rang, she was sure she was going to faint. This was it. Sam had arrived. There was no going back.

Heather walked slowly to the door and opened it. And there was Sam Moon, standing tall and strapping in her doorway. He was, of course, nothing but a big blur. She only had her visual memories to go on, so she projected a past image of Sam onto the blur that stood before her and imagined him in a tuxedo. It made for a stunningly gorgeous image. All those little curls of reddish brown hair that she'd always adored, and that perfectly sculpted Apollo-like face that she'd sometimes just stared at while he slept. It actually made the moment more emotional than she had planned. Without the vision to inform her present, she could only sink further and further into the past, and memories of Sam started flooding her brain. This was a moment that had once occurred with great regularity: Sam showing up at her door to take her out for a date. To the movies, to dinner, to his dorm...

She raised the black handkerchief to her head and began to dab incessantly.

"You made it," she said, smiling insecurely.

Sam didn't respond, and her nerves doubled. God, did she look like a fool? Had her mother dressed her up in some sort of JC Penney getup from hell?

"Wow...," Sam uttered finally.

"What?" Heather moaned. "Is it awful? My mom did it. It's all her fault."

"I just forgot that you were so... You look amazing."

"I do?"

"You truly do, Heather."

Hearing him in person was a completely different experience from the phone. She suddenly remembered that Sam's voice at such close proximity had this uncommon quality. Whenever he said something, it was abundantly clear that he meant it. Her stomach finally dropped back down to its appropriate position, and she grinned with relief.

"Thanks," she breathed. "My mom did it."

"So I hear."

"Right." She laughed. "Sorry. I would tell you how handsome you look, but I'm afraid it's all a blur."

"Well, you look good enough for both of us," he said. "So, are you ready to go?"

"Yes," she said with a definitive nod. "I just need to get my bag."

Unfortunately, it ended up not being that simple. Heather tried to retrieve her bag and make it out with a goodbye yell to her parents, but her mother and father were both armed and ready with cameras. Prom night was, of course, an inescapable parental photo op, and she supposed, given everything her family had been through, they deserved it.

She hated forcing Sam to endure the seemingly interminable poses and flashbulbs, but he handled it with nothing but kindness, grace, and charm, and it was ultimately pretty painless. Finally, after a long, tearful bear hug, her mother permitted their official release, and Sam and Heather made their way to the elevator and down to the street.

They walked out of her lobby, and Heather immediately found herself disconcerted by the blur of lights and sounds. The city was still a bit much for her to handle after living in the quiet safety of Carverton. She took an unconscious step back toward her building and found herself yearning once more for some assisted living.

"Are you okay?" Sam asked.

"Uh-huh," she said meekly. "It's all just a little. . . overwhelming. The lights kind of blur together into one big ball."

But Sam stepped closer and placed his fingers through hers, gripping her hand with more assurance and security than any of the trained professionals at school had ever managed.

"Don't worry," he said. "I'll lead." He leaned over and kissed her cheek just below her ear. A bolt of tingles ran down her spine. She had to force herself to remember that this was *not* that kind of date—which wasn't so easy to do when Sam Moon held your hand and kissed you on the cheek. There was an awkward pause.

"I know," Sam said. "This is a little weird."

He apparently could also read minds.

"A little bit," she admitted, dabbing her forehead again. "I think you may be a little too remarkable for a purely platonic date."

Sam laughed. "Shut up."

"I'm serious," Heather insisted. "I don't know what Gaia was thinking when she let you slip away. . . ." Heather cringed. She had most definitely not meant to say that out loud. She prayed that she hadn't just blown this date and wished to God that she could take back what she'd said. There was definitely a much too extensive, much too awkward silence that followed.

"Tell you what," Sam said. He took hold of both her hands. "Let's not worry about Gaia tonight, okay? Knowing Gaia, I can't quite picture her attending a prom anyway. I guess this is a little weird, you and me together. But you know what?"

"What?"

"I don't really care how weird it is. I'm glad you asked me to this thing. I think we should just enjoy this night. I think we should celebrate the fact that you and I are standing here right now, alive and 'sort of' seeing." He leaned forward as if to check on the status of her eyesight.

Heather laughed. He had found just the right way to put her at ease. She felt a thick lump building in her throat, but she swallowed it down. "Yes," she agreed. That was as much as she could manage to say right now.

"Yes?"

"Yes," she repeated with a confident smile.

"Good." Sam gave her hands a strong squeeze. "Now, about five steps away there is a beautiful luxury sedan waiting to whisk us off to the prom in style. And if you stick close, I will make damn sure that you do not bang your head on the way in. Shall we?" He tucked her arm tightly within his and led the way. And with each step, Heather began to feel more and more like herself. Her new self.

ED KEPT TRYING TO FOCUS HIS BRAIN

Pretty in Pink

on the moment. He couldn't let his mind fall down that slippery slope toward the past—toward regret and stupid stale fantasies of what "should have been." If he could stay in the moment, then maybe he could enjoy it. He could find the pleasure in this prom thing if he really pushed. He was sure of it. Kai was a great girl! School had been swell! And now it was time to dance, dance, dance!

Jesus. You're pathetic.

Dance, dance, dance. If that was the best Ed could drum up for end-of-the-year inspiration, he was truly screwed.

He had to stop trying to fake the inspiration. That would get him absolutely nowhere. He'd have to count on Kai. He'd count on her upbeat attitude and her all-around joie de vivre. She had a contagious smile and a contagious spirit. Kai was the secret. Kai would pump him right up for sure.

Ed picked up the pace and turned the corner for Kai's building. She had wholeheartedly agreed with him in their last phone call that they should meet downstairs to avoid the giant bear trap that was the parental photo op. Ed's mother had already snapped plenty of shots of him in his tux at home, and Kai's parents had already subjected her to a full solo photo shoot as well. So that was done.

He walked the few steps to Kai's buzzer, and then he held up for one last smile-practice session. He at least owed Kai a nice fat smile. The last thing he wanted to do was let his nagging prom ambivalence rub off on her. She deserved to have the time of her life, even if Ed had to fake it a little. Once he'd given his jaw a nice workout, he breathed deep, punched the buzzer to her apartment, and waited.

Her voice trumpeted through the blaring intercom, nearly knocking him back a step. "I'll be right down!"

Okay, Ed. Relax, breathe, enjoy. Relax, breathe, enjoy. This is a monumental rite of passage in your young teenage life. These are the good times. These are the days of wine and roses. Celebrate the moments of your life. Don't worry, be happy. Carpe diem. Life is a highway, you want to ride it all night long. . . . Um. . .

Nope. He had run out of inspirational song lyrics and platitudes. It had been worth a try, though. No, it was definitely up to Kai now.

He stepped down to the street and backed up to the curb so that he could take in her grand entrance from a good cinematic perspective. He would try to pump up the music in his head and experience her entrance in slow motion. That would give it that teen movie spark for sure. That would fill his empty heart right up with "coming-of-age" delight.

He saw the first glimpse of Kai's pink shoes through the window of her building as she clomped down the stairs. Then a glimpse of her pink dress and then the neon pink barrettes dangling throughout her hair. Okay, she had clearly been watching *Pretty in Pink* in preparation for the prom and gotten inspired.

But that was *good*. That was good. That was what Ed was looking for here. You couldn't get more "teen movie" than John Hughes. And nothing screamed, "Prom is the most important moment of your life," like *Pretty in Pink*.

Okay. This is good. This is good.

Ed searched his comprehensive movie-trivia memory banks for the right music to play in his head. Pretty in Pink. *Eighties teen movie staple. Genre defining. Who did the song. . . ? Some eighties freak band. . .*

Psychedelic Furs. That was it. The Psychedelic Furs singing "Pretty in Pink."

Ed started running the song through his head.

Isn't sheee. . .

Pretty in pink. . .

Isn't she?

Ed turned up the tune in his head as Kai swung open the door. He slowed the entire moment down to slow motion, watching as Kai stepped out onto the stoop, her tutulike pink dress blowing in the wind, her barrettes dangling from her hair like neon candy, her glorious smile lighting up the darkened street. She truly was a vision. A ray of bright pink light in a cold, harsh universe. The coolest, cutest thing he'd ever seen. The sweetest girl in the world. A good, good friend.

But something went wrong. His subconscious stepped in out of nowhere like a little demon—a tiny little emotional saboteur creeping in to change his vision. He couldn't even control it. The new vision was rolling out in slow motion, and he was powerless to stop it. . . .

Suddenly her pink dress began to turn black in his mind's eye. Black, and sleeker, and more sophisticated. The barrettes dropped from her head. Her petite little body began to sprout up and stretch out into a taut, warriorlike frame. Her rounded cheeks became sculpted and angular like a Viking goddess's. Her Kewpie doll smile shifted into a smoldering frown. Her brown eyes turned a heavenly shade of aqua blue, and finally, her short brown hair grew into a mess of long dirty-blond tendrils, cascading down her face onto her bare cream-colored shoulders.

Gaia. Gaia was stepping down the stairs, ready for Ed to escort her to the prom.

Cut. Stop the tape. Kill the music. Stop it, Ed. Drain it, flush it, stomp it out of your head.

Ed shook the stupid vision from his head and refocused his eyes on reality. On Kai. The lovely Kai.

"Are you okay?" Kai was staring at him with concern. "You look weird."

"I'm fine," he assured her. "I'm great! God, look at you. You look beautiful."

Kai grinned from ear to ear. "Really?"

"*Hell*, yes," he bellowed. He gave Kai an overly enthusiastic hug, trying to shake the Gaia demons from his subversive subconscious. "Are you ready to rock?"

"Oh my God," she said, grabbing Ed's shoulders. "We are going to rock so hard."

"I'll get us a cab," Ed said. He grabbed Kai's hand and guided her down the street as she clomped in her platform shoes to keep up.

Get her out of your head, he hollered at himself, keeping the smile pasted on his face.

He had to do it. He had to shake these stupid outdated visions of the end of high school. Wasn't that the point? That was the entire point of graduating. It was time to *stop* living in a high school world of adolescent fantasies and start learning how to live in the *real* world out there. Gaia and Ed together at the prom was no longer part of the real world.

Still, he couldn't help thinking. . . .

Somewhere out there in the real world, there was a guy who *was* Gaia's date for the evening. And he was a lucky man.

CHRIS HAD DARED TO SNEAK OUT

in public just so he could purchase himself a new outfit at Ralph Lauren. He wanted to look as manly, serious, and well tailored as possible for his meeting with General Colter. He'd obviously gotten the general's attention with his little demonstration, but now he needed to seal the

Hideous Orange Jumpsuits

deal against his father and Skyler. He needed Colter to take him seriously, and given their last meeting, where he'd "poured on the gay," he needed an outfit to counter the image. Ralph Lauren was the most ungay designer he could think of without appearing completely unfashionable. A black jacket and turtleneck seemed to fit the bill.

He tried to dampen his excitement as he approached the vacant lot on West Twelfth Street, but it was hard to keep his swelling pride in check.

Because he was *winning*. His plan had worked.

What do you think, Dad? Beating you and Skyler at your own game? Man enough for you? Ever think there was a reason I was a two-time city chess champ? Checkmate, assholes.

He couldn't wait to watch their whole plan go public. He couldn't wait to watch them on the local news, trying to hide their faces from the cameras (for *once*) as they were hauled into custody by men in black suits and aviator sunglasses. He could hear the news report already. . . .

Another shocking corporate scandal today as billionaire Robert Rodke and his son Skyler were indicted for serious drug crimes, including attempts to defraud the U.S. government. . .

It was all just beautiful. Maybe he would visit them a few times in white-collar prison—take a little walk with them on the fenced-in grounds, Chris in street clothes, his brother and father in those hideous orange jumpsuits. Perhaps he'd ask them who was the smart one now? Who was getting the respect now? Probably not the guy in the orange jumpsuit, right, Skyler?

Chris did begin to get a little spooked as he approached the vacant lot. He'd picked out this location in sunny daylight, but by 9 p.m., it was more than a little sketchy. He could just imagine Jake waiting for him in this little hellhole last night, spooked out of his mind. Though that was nothing compared to the heart attack Jake must have had when that army of Droogs attacked. Chris knew it would have been too dangerous for him to be anywhere near the scene, and now he was glad he'd decided to stay at the hotel for the entire "demonstration." It would have been too ugly to watch.

Poor Jake. Chris wondered who had found his body and hauled it off to the morgue. Colter had probably placed the 911 call anonymously. That's what Chris figured would have happened. He couldn't believe there'd been nothing in the news about the "brutal murder of an innocent teen." Maybe the news folks were just getting tired of reporting another "ultraviolent" Droog crime. No matter. All that mattered now was getting Colter's attention. And Chris had done that quite successfully.

He walked into the center of the lot, trying to keep his fear in check. Now he could see the dark brown bloodstains all over the pavement. All that dried-up blood, just barely illuminated by the two shattered streetlights on each corner. *Ugh.* He could just picture last night's carnage. It was downright disturbing. Ordering a murder was one thing, but seeing the actual aftermath made him nauseous. Chris wanted out of this lot as soon as possible.

He checked his watch. 9:10. He was surprised. He couldn't believe that a man like General Colter would ever be late. It just went to show, you could never judge a book by its cover. Even a buttoned-up military man like Colter could be a flake.

Finally Chris heard footsteps approaching. Thank God. This lot was just way too creepy to spend another minute alone in it.

"It's about time," Chris called out, moving toward the corner to meet up with the general. But as the approaching figure moved into the light, Chris began to realize...

It wasn't the general.

"You're goddamn right, it's about time," the figure said.

"*Jake?*" Chris's eyes nearly popped out of their sockets. Jake was standing in the one shaft of light at the entrance to the lot. His face was covered in cuts and bruises. His left hand was wrapped in a heavy bandage. But he was unquestionably alive.

"Surprised?" Jake asked. He began to walk toward Chris at a brisk pace. "You look incredibly surprised to see me, Chris. Why is that?"

Suddenly a pack of men in gray suits came pouring out of the dark alley in the corner—every one of them with a gun pointed straight at Chris's face. His heart leapt into his throat. He took no time to think. There was no time to make sense of any of this. He just needed to run, and fast.

Chris swung around and took off for the street, his designer shoes pounding on the pavement as he heaved for breath. He whipped his head around to look behind him as the men in gray closed in on him. He darted his eyes from side to side and tried to pick a direction to run. He took off down a side street and headed for the highway. He could find a tunnel down there—an alley to duck into, a trash bin to hide in, anything. He whipped his face back forward, and that's when it hit him.

The sound of a screeching car pierced his eardrums. A huge block of black metal flashed before his eyes, smashing into him like a freight train, sending shocks of excruciating pain through every bone in his body as he was hurled backward like a rag doll against the rock-hard street. He cried out in pain as his head bashed against the ground. He flattened his scraped-up hands against the street and tried to push his aching body back up, but there was already a man standing overhead, jabbing the cold metal of a gun barrel straight into the center of Chris's forehead.

"Do *not* move!" the man growled into his face. "If you even *attempt* to move, I will blow your head clean off." Chris could barely make out the man's features. All he could see were his graying temples and his ice blue eyes, burning with rage.

The men in gray caught up and surrounded Chris on the ground, staring down at him with cold, heartless expressions, like a group of surgeons. And then Jake leaned in overhead, like the doctor who was about to make the first incision.

"All right, get up!" the man with the blue eyes ordered. He jammed his fingers into Chris's chest, bunching his shirt up in a fist and dragging him up off the street. Then he slammed Chris's back up against the side of a black limousine. Now Chris could see the open black car door he'd collided with.

"In the car, *now!*" the man ordered. It wasn't as if Chris had a choice. The man grabbed the back of Chris's head and shoved him into the car, scraping his face along the hard leather seat. Then he shoved Chris up against the window, keeping the gun to his head. Jake got into the car and slammed the door.

"Jake," Chris croaked. "What's going—?"

"Don't talk!" the man hollered. He jabbed the gun against Chris's head, sending a bolt of exquisite pain down his neck. "You're done talking. You don't talk until I tell you to talk, do you understand?"

Chris shut his mouth and prayed silently for his life.

Gaia had to admit, it was good **stone— cold** wine. At least they **princess** were trying to send her out in style.

GAIA WAS STARING AT A HIDEOUS

The Underworld

pink flaky mass, also known as a pâté cracker. There were six of them on a plate sitting on Skyler's dining table, staring back at her like little pink demons beckoning her down to the underworld.

Poison? Was that how he wanted to do it? Poison pâté? Did he really think he could bump her off with appetizers? *Try again, Skyler. You'll have to do better than that.*

He had enlisted every single romantic cliché in the book for their "big adult dinner," also known as "Substitute Prom Night." He had turned off all the lights in the apartment and lit a bunch of candles. He had laid out a big luxurious spread of fine wine and gourmet cheese and, of course, pâté. He'd even put on the soft R & B music. She was half expecting him to come out of the kitchen in a satin playboy robe, smoking from a long cigarette holder. She pitied the numerous girls who had probably fallen for this crap in the past. Naive freshman college girls who had spent their lives drinking wine coolers in the mall parking lot and thought that good wine and a good name somehow indicated a man they could trust.

But Gaia was as far from trusting as a girl could

possibly get. Her body and mind were on high alert. She was watching him like an eagle. Focusing her exceptional vision on every move he made, every gesture. When was it coming? How was it coming? She was waiting for it. She was waiting for him to make his move.

The more she looked around, the more she realized that it didn't even look like a date. The big spread on the dining table, all those flickering candles in the darkness. . . It looked like a wake. Her wake. Her "last supper," they were surely thinking. God, did they really think she was this stupid? Did they really think she was so gullible that they could take her out without her even seeing it coming?

Of course they did. She hadn't given them any evidence to the contrary, had she? They'd successfully transformed her into a pathetic girlie-girl eating right out of the palm of their hands. Her face began to burn with embarrassment as she thought about that girl she'd become. Thank God that was over. Thank God she was *her* again, or they would probably be examining the internal organs of her corpse at this very moment.

Skyler floated out of the kitchen in his stretch black T-shirt and a pair of black silk pants. How polite of him to wear black to her wake. He placed two wineglasses on the dining table. "Hey," he complained. "You haven't even tried the pâté yet. You've *got* to try this. My dad has it flown in from Paris. It's the best there is."

He picked up the demon cracker, guarding it from dropping with his other hand, and he raised it to Gaia's mouth. Gaia sealed her jaw shut.

"What's wrong?" he asked.

Smile, Gaia. Smile, goddamn it.

She turned up the corners of her mouth. "Gee, I don't know," she mumbled girlishly. "I'm not really a pâté person. I'm more of a Gray's Papaya girl."

"What's Gray's Papaya?"

Jesus, she really had been out of her mind, hadn't she? She'd been spending days and days with a man who didn't even know what Gray's Papaya was.

She took the cracker in her hands and stared at it.

"It's delicious," he assured her. "I promise."

"I'm *scared.*" She giggled. "Okay, if it's so delicious, prove it." Translation: *If it's not poison, prove it.* She raised the cracker to his mouth to feed it to him.

He locked his eyes with hers for a moment. Then he grinned and opened wide, taking the entire cracker in one bite, letting his lips linger on her finger with voracious sexual fervor.

Gaia was dying inside. Her skin was crawling. *Ew. Just. . . ew.* But at least she had struck poison pâté from the list of potential murder weapons.

"Mmm," he crooned. "Delicious. Here, try the wine." He uncorked the bottle and poured them each half a glass, handing one to her. Fine. The wine had been sealed. She would trust the wine. Besides, poison was most likely not the way they would go. "Wait," he said. "A toast..."

This she wanted to hear. She grinned and held up her glass.

"To finally being free of the high school shackles," he said. "To graduating to full-on adulthood. To your future..."

"No," she corrected him. "To *our* future." As in her continued heartbeat and his life behind bars.

"Yes," he agreed. "To our future."

They clinked glasses and took their sips, and then Skyler placed their glasses back on the table. Gaia had to admit, it was good wine. At least they were trying to send her out in style.

He suddenly grabbed her wrist with his strong fingers. Gaia's other hand instantly clenched into a fist at her side, armed and ready to dismantle his face. *I do hope you're kidding,* she howled at him silently. *You want to go hand-to-hand? That's the plan? You must be out of your mind. I'll break your neck in one blow.*

"I want to show you something." He beamed excitedly. "Speaking of the future... come here."

Gaia quickly relaxed her fist and her breathing, hoping he hadn't noticed. So, it wouldn't be hand-to-hand combat. Apparently he was not, in fact, that stupid. So *what,* then? When was it coming? Skyler dragged her over to his desk and pulled an envelope out of a drawer, handing it to her.

"What's this?" she asked.

"Open it." He smiled.

She let her eyes linger on his, and then she ripped open the envelope and pulled out a pamphlet-sized folder with the blue Continental Airlines logo on the front. She turned to him dubiously.

"Keep opening," he encouraged her.

She opened the folder and pulled out a plane ticket in her name. Destination: Key West, Florida. Her spine stiffened with anger. Of course. Get her prints on the ticket. Leave a nice clear paper trail for her sudden disappearance. They really were covering all their bases. She plastered on a look of elated surprise.

"Oh my God!" she shouted. "You didn't."

"I did."

"*Skyler*. You are so. . . *sweet*. You didn't have to do this." She forced herself to hug him gratefully. "But. . . how come there's only one?" *Answer that one, asshole.* She knew the real answer. He couldn't book a companion ticket in his name or the police would know exactly which door to knock on first. That would point a finger directly at the Rodkes.

"I didn't want to be presumptuous," he said. "But if you'd like a companion. . . I can call the travel agency tomorrow. They've got my ticket on hold." He grinned sheepishly.

"Cute," she said. "Very cute." In the ugliest possible way.

He ran his finger along the side of her face. "Stay here," he said. "I'll be right back. Nature calls." He left her standing by the desk and walked down the hall to the bathroom. Gaia didn't skip a beat. She slammed the ticket down on the desk and moved with silent feline quickness to the bathroom door. She had no intention of leaving him unattended for even a moment. She pressed her hands to the door frame and listened closely. And sure enough, she could hear him speaking. Most likely into his cell phone. But he was speaking in such a whisper that even her highly attuned ears couldn't pick up the words. She whipped around and slithered back to her position at the desk, waiting for his return.

"You know what?" he announced, prancing back into the room. "I just had myself a little brainstorm."

"Oh, *do* tell."

"Well. . ." He picked up the wine and tucked it under his arm, grabbing the two glasses between the fingers of one hand and picking up the plate of pâté in the other. "It has turned out to be such a beautiful night. I think we should take this party to the roof." He turned to her. "What do you think?"

Gaia stared at him long and hard. "I think that's a great idea." She smiled.

"Well, then, off we go." He walked over and held out his elbow for her to take. She placed her arm through his as if she couldn't be more delighted. As if they were off to see the Wizard.

But now she knew. The roof. Whatever it was, it was going to happen on the roof. And she was ready.

Childlike Tears

OLIVER'S FINGERS WERE SUFFOCATING the handle of his gun. He was digging a small crimson impression into Chris Rodke's forehead with the barrel. He knew that it was essential time to control one's temper while holding a gun, but the images in his head were telling a different story. He wanted to decimate this kid. He wanted to splatter his brains all over the car window. He wanted to see him bleed. But he had to maintain control. He had to keep his finger off the trigger. Because he needed the information.

His trap had worked to perfection. With that soldier's one overheard conversation, he'd been able to contrive a perfectly plausible fake e-mail from this General Colter to Chris. All he'd needed was a fake e-mail address and for Chris to take the bait, which he'd obviously been young and stupid enough to do.

175

Now he had Chris where he wanted him, and he had no intention of wasting any more time. The city was racing by them through the window, and Gaia was out there somewhere. He needed to know where they were going. He needed an address for his driver in the next sixty seconds.

"Tell us where Gaia is," Oliver demanded.

Chris looked at Jake with deep confusion. "Jake, who is this guy? What happened to you? Did he do this to you?"

"Shut up!" Jake snapped. "Don't waste your time lying, Chris. I know you set me up. Just tell us where she is. We know she's with your brother."

"Where's General Colter?" Chris asked.

"*I* wrote the e-mail, you idiot." Oliver smacked the gun into Chris's head again, bumping him against the car window. "And you're going to tell me who this General Colter is and what the military has to do with your family's plans. You're going to tell me everything *after* you give me your brother's location. Now."

"Who are you?" Chris squawked.

"I am Gaia Moore's uncle, and you have screwed with the wrong family. Now stop asking questions and start answering them or I will unload this entire cartridge into your face."

"All right, all right!" Chris held out his hands. "I'll tell you where she is."

"Good."

"If you let me out of this car."

Oliver's eyes widened. "What did you say?"

"I said, let me out of the car, and I'll tell you where she is."

Oliver's hands began to tremble with frustration. He grabbed the lapels of Chris's jacket and tugged him closer. "This is not a negotiation. We are not *bargaining* here, you little—"

"Look, I'm sorry," Chris interrupted, "but we *are* bargaining. You need to know where she is. I'm the only one who can tell you where she is. If you kill me, you have nothing, so *I* set the terms, right? If you stop the car and let me out, *then,* and only then, will I tell you where Gaia is. It's really that simple."

Oliver stared into Chris's defiant little eyes and something inside him just snapped. He felt it happen. He felt the last vestiges of his patience implode in his head. He shook Chris's entire body like a scarecrow, rocking him back and forth again and again until even he was dizzy. Then he shoved his gun deep into Chris's mouth. His hand was shaking with rage, knocking the gun against Chris's teeth. "You cocky little bastard. You think I care whether you live or die? I don't care." He pushed the gun to the back of his throat until Chris began to gag. "You really are an imbecile, aren't you? You just signed your own death certificate." Oliver cocked the gun and brought his finger to the trigger.

"Oliver, don't!" Jake shouted. He reached for

Oliver's arm, but Oliver shoved him back in his seat. "Don't!" Jake pleaded. "Jesus, we need him to tell us where she is. We don't want to kill anyone, we just need to know where she is—"

"Shut up!" Oliver shouted. "Just shut up, Jake! I'll find her myself. This little bastard is dead." Oliver shoved Chris up against the window and pulled the trigger halfway back.

Chris cried out helplessly, flailing his arms forward in surrender, coughing violently. Tears were suddenly dripping from the corners of his eyes. He was trying to form words.

"Wait!" Jake hollered. "Just wait, wait! He's trying to talk—"

"He had his chance."

Chris's cries jumped an octave to a simpering whine. "I'll tell you," he was trying to say with the gun stuck in his mouth. "I'll tell you where she is."

"Oliver, *calm* down," Jake begged. "*Please.* Please don't do this. . . ."

Oliver froze in place. His heart was pounding like a hammer. Adrenaline was coursing through his veins like bolts of electric current. He had one desire and one desire only: to shoot this boy in the face. Shoot to kill.

But he stared long and hard into the boy's eyes. And he finally took a breath. He breathed in, and he breathed out. And then he pulled the gun slowly from Chris's mouth and placed it back in its holster.

"I'll tell you," Chris cried, finally able to speak clearly. "I swear to God. I swear. . . ." Chris pulled his knees up against his chest. He coughed painfully and shielded his face to hide his childlike tears. He tried in vain to catch his breath.

Oliver pushed himself back against the seat, trying to regain his sense of reason. It was like he had been in some kind of trance state. It was like trying to recover from a bout with demonic possession.

He had nearly done something completely irrational. He had come within centimeters of killing the one person who could get him to Gaia. He'd been ready to strike down yet another child young enough to be his son. Just as he had done to Sam Moon. Just as he had done to Mary Moss and to Josh. Just as he had nearly done to Jake the day before.

It was the first time he had really come to terms with the truth. Oliver Moore was entirely gone. And Loki was all that remained.

MEGAN FELT LIKE A STONE-COLD

Royal Occasion

princess. She couldn't help it. She just knew her "look" was firing on all pistons tonight. She stepped slowly out of the limo, making sure to show off her perfectly waxed legs and her four-hundred-dollar Prada shoes, and then she waited on the brightly lit sidewalk, smoothing out her black Hermés scarf and gazing through the glass doors of the Supper Club.

She checked behind her to make sure that her date looked as elegant as she did. Rob Preston was her prince for the evening. He looked damn fine in his tux, and thankfully, he'd gotten an excellent haircut. Not that his hair was his best quality. His best quality by far was his body, which was cut like a Greek god's—pretty much a requirement for the captain of the football team, which was the closest thing to a prince that high school had to offer. They were perfectly matched for this royal occasion.

Megan's heart raced with excitement as Melanie and the ladies gathered on either side of her and they began their supermodel strut down the small red carpet that led into the club. How perfectly appropriate that the carpet be red. She could just imagine a slew of paparazzi lining up on either side of them, blocked off by velvet ropes, flashing away and calling out their names, desperately trying to get their heads to turn for a good shot. *Megan, over here! Melanie, give us a smile. . . !* After all, how often was it that five stone-cold princesses could be captured in one shot? This would probably be the last time.

As they entered the lobby, Megan could already

hear the pounding bass drum and the din of the crowd through the doors of the club. Perfect. Their fashionable lateness couldn't have been better timed. The party was already in full effect—which was just what the girls had wanted. They had come here to turn some heads, and that required that everyone be there when they burst through the doors like superstars.

The girls all checked their coats, letting the boys handle the tickets while they gave each other one last once-over before their grand entrance.

Megan turned to Melanie first, as her opinion was the one that really counted. "Mel? Hair?"

"Perfecto," Melanie replied, flashing the "okay" sign. "Lipstick?" She flashed her teeth to Megan for a smear check.

"Pearly," she replied with a thumbs-up.

"Wrinkles?" Tammie asked, smoothing out her skintight Versace dress.

"Not a one," Laurie said.

"Oh my God, you guys!" Trish shook her fists with excitement. "This is it. This is *our* prom!"

They all hooted in unison.

Megan gave them all one last looking over and then she was satisfied. "Ladies? I do believe we look hot. Are we ready to head in there and greet our royal subjects?"

"Ready," they confirmed with a giggle.

"Then let's do this." Megan tugged her prince by

her side, and they headed for the gold-trimmed royal blue doors. The ladies grabbed their dates and followed suit. They strutted to the two separate sets of double doors, gave each other one last nod, and then they swung open the doors to the sudden roar of the music.

"Ladies and gentlemen!" Megan shouted. "We have arrived!" She threw her hand on her hip and flashed a massive grin, secretly waiting for the heads to turn en masse.

But no heads turned. In fact, most of the heads were turned in the other direction.

It seemed like half the senior class had all gathered around one table. They were practically lined up, as if someone was handing out free beers or something. Megan craned her head to try and see what was up at that table. Who could possibly be drawing that much attention?

"Who *is* that?" Melanie asked, sounding perturbed. She stepped next to Megan to try and get a better view.

"No way," Rob said as a smile spread over his face. He let go of Megan's arm and stepped directly in front of her, as if she weren't even there. "Is that Heather?"

"It totally is," Brad agreed. "Heather freaking Gannis. Heather's back. We gotta say hello. . . ."

Rob and the boys all trotted quickly down the steps, joining the crowd for Heather's one-woman receiving line. Megan and the girls were left standing at the doorway alone.

The girls just stood there in awkward silence. Now Megan could see Heather, seated in her chair in a black strapless dress, giving out huge gracious smiles, handshakes, hugs, and kisses to each of her adoring fans one by one. She looked like. . .

She looked like a queen.

"Heather's back. . . ," Laurie uttered. "Wow."

"Yeah," Tammie breathed. "That's. . . That's awesome."

"Yeah," Melanie agreed. "Definitely."

They continued to stand there in silence.

"Well, why are we all standing here?" Tracee finally asked. "I mean, we should go say hello."

"Yeah," Megan agreed, still not moving. "We definitely should." She turned back to Melanie. "Do we have to wait in the line?"

"I don't know," Melanie said, pondering the question.

Slowly but surely the girls began to split off from each other one by one. And they got in line. Megan was the last to follow. She watched as the girls got lost in the huge crowd of Heather's delighted royal subjects.

Megan still felt like a princess. She did. She reminded herself that she *was* one. Or at least. . . she looked like one. They were *all* princesses—every one of them. But Heather. . .

Heather was most definitely the queen.

THERE WASN'T ONE STAR IN THE

desolate New York sky. It was like stepping out into a gaping black hole. Like the entire building was floating in darkness. It somehow made the roof even more claustrophobic

Dark Black Void

than Skyler's apartment. What could he possibly do to her up here? Up in this empty void? Gaia couldn't think of a thing. And that was shaking her confidence for the first time "Come on," he said. "Over here."

He walked ahead of her to the edge of the roof and placed the wine and food down on the waist-high ledge. Gaia found herself staying put at the center of the roof, by the brick partition under the water tank. It wasn't that she was scared to walk farther. It was just that she was wary. She needed to watch her back now, and the edge of the roof felt way too exposed from all sides. She couldn't help but wonder if there were snipers out there in the black fog—somewhere in the shadows of one of the adjacent roofs or aiming from one of the hundreds of darkened windows that surrounded them.

"Gaia." Skyler laughed. "*Over here.* Come on." He refilled her glass with wine and held it out for her. She could hardly make out his face. He was just a gray figure in the shadow, barely lit in silhouette by the city lights below.

184

"Right. I'm just. . . a little afraid of heights," she lied.

"Well, don't worry," he said. "I won't let you fall."

She had no choice. She had to keep bluffing until they showed their cards. No attempted murder meant no arrest. And that meant that the Rodkes would continue to roam free. Free to keep finding new and inventive ways to exploit her and destroy her. She'd already been through the cycle enough times with Loki to know: Her enemies never gave up unless they were dead or behind bars. As long as they were free, she never would be. And that was no longer acceptable. This time she had to wipe the slate clean.

She bit the bullet and gave up her position, walking out to him to accept her wine. She took a quick sip and then placed her glass back down on the ledge. She wanted to be sure to have both hands free at all times. Skyler put his glass down, too, and then he wrapped his arm around her shoulders and breathed in the air.

"Isn't it beautiful up here?" he asked.

"Uh-huh," Gaia replied. She looked out across the sea of black tar roofs and water tanks and chimneys. In a way, she supposed it was sort of beautiful. Beautiful in its supreme stillness and desolation. An entire cityscape done in charcoal—everything in various shades of black and gray.

But any beauty she'd found in this ugly moment was immediately ripped away. Skyler suddenly dropped his hand from her shoulder and clamped down on her arms with brute force. He was so much faster than she'd expected. He'd literally caught her off balance, sending her stumbling back toward the edge of the roof. She quickly clamped her hands on the ledge and glued her feet to the ground as Skyler forced his body against hers, digging the stone ledge harder and harder into the base of her spine. She couldn't even tell what he was trying to do. Was he trying to throw her off the roof, or was he trying to kiss her? She wasn't even sure which fate would be worse.

But it was neither.

The first hint of a noise sent Gaia's eyes darting over Skyler's shoulder, zeroing in on the brick partition at the center of the roof. There was something behind that wall, and it was moving. They weren't alone.

"They won't hurt you," Skyler whispered. "It'll be quick and painless."

Suddenly they were pouring out of the darkness like a pack of white ghosts. All these men—huge, ugly men in white hospital scrubs—storming out from behind the brick partition, careening toward her. They were each holding something. What were they holding? Guns? Knives? It was so dark. They halted just behind Skyler and waited with anticipation. It was like they were waiting for him to give the order. Gaia could finally see their hands. She could see what they were holding. Not guns or knives. . .

Syringes. Needles the size of daggers in every

hand—their thumbs pressed to the plungers and ready. Lethal injection? Was that the plan?

"They just need to give you a little shot," Skyler said. "It won't hurt a bit. So, don't be scared, okay?"

Scared? Any other girl in the world would have known instantly that she was doomed. There were so many of them. At least ten massive sons of bitches ready to shoot her up with poison. Any other girl would have just leaned back and let herself plummet from that roof rather than face the slow death of a lethal injection and the dissection of her corpse that would follow. But Gaia wasn't any other girl. And she was thinking something very different. . . .

Finally, she celebrated. *It's about freaking time.*

The Rodkes had finally shown their cards. And Gaia wasn't remotely impressed with their hand. The fact that they hadn't even come with real weapons of any kind was insulting enough, but worse than that, these big, strapping meatheads looked like orderlies. *Scared?* She turned back to Skyler and looked him dead in the eyes.

"See, the thing is. . ." She leaned her mouth to his ear as if she were telling him a secret. Which she was. A secret that she had been patiently waiting for the right time to reveal. "I'm not scared," she whispered. "I'm not scared at all."

God, how long had she been waiting for this moment? She grabbed Skyler's wrist, jabbed her elbow deep into his ribs, and then hurled him over her back, watching his body sail to the ground and skid across the tar and gravel. The orderlies didn't skip a beat. The second they saw their boss get thrown to the ground, they stormed in for the attack.

Gaia whirled around to face them, and her mind instantly snapped into combat mode. It was the most crystal-clear state of consciousness, a glorious mix of electric energy and pure relaxation. Only now did she realize how very much she had missed this feeling while it was away. This feeling was who she was. This feeling defined her.

But enough about feelings. A syringe was sailing for her arm. She twirled in the air with a high-flying roundhouse kick that knocked the syringe right out of her assailant's hand. She followed instantly with a scissor kick to his fat face that snapped his neck back and knocked him unconscious. The moment she landed, she dropped to her knees, ducking another swing, and then she shot out her leg with a whip-fast sweeping kick that knocked two more of them on their asses.

She popped back to her feet, her knees bent and ready for more. She *wanted* more. She needed it.

Two of them converged on her from either side. She ducked down again and let their heads collide with the most hideous cracking noise. They were down for the count.

The more she saw of those white scrubs, the more

she began to flash back to her days in that hellhole in Florida. She grew more vengeful with every blow. The next one went for her leg, but she zeroed in on his windpipe and snapped a high kick to his neck that sent him crashing to the ground, gurgling as he gasped for air. He would pass out in a few more seconds.

Six down, four to go. God, she wished there were more of them.

Three more barreled toward her clumsily. She pinpointed the left one's wrist as he swung toward her, and she grabbed it on the way down, rocking him completely off balance and dislocating his arm in the process. He howled with pain as she used all of his clumsy momentum to hurl him over her shoulder and send him flying into the other two like a three-hundred-pound cannonball.

That left only one, and she wanted to make it count. He growled as he ran toward her, as if his war cry would somehow increase his power. He aimed his syringe for the center of her chest. Gaia let out a deep guttural shout of her own, straight from her center, just as her father had taught her. She ran for the edge of the roof, using the ledge as a springboard that shot her back toward him with twice the speed and twice the power. She sailed through the air and let out a deep, cathartic grunt as her foot connected with his face. The blow sent his entire body sailing backward. His head was the first thing to hit the ground. It smacked the gravel with a deadly thud.

And then there were none.

Gaia landed squarely on her feet and took in a deep breath. Then she turned around, looking past all the white-clad bodies on the ground, and she fixed her eyes on Skyler Rodke. He was sitting comfortably with his back against the ledge and his arms draped over his knees, as if he'd just been hanging out and watching a really good kung fu movie.

"Wow." He shook his head with amazement. "That was just. . . God*damn*, that was impressive."

"Was that *it?*" Gaia scoffed, staring at him in the dark. "Was that the whole plan, right there?" She wanted to stare him down. She wanted to stare him down until he begged for mercy just from looking into her vengeful eyes. She wanted to walk straight up to him and kick him square in the face. The only problem was. . . she was having more and more trouble seeing him. Because she was beginning to brown out. Her limbs suddenly felt like tissue paper blowing in the wind.

Jesus. It had been so long. It had been so long since a fight like this. She'd been so anxious to do battle, she'd completely neglected to consider the aftermath. *The postbattle blackout.* She hadn't used her fuel like this in so long, and now that she was done fighting, her tank was flat-out empty. Not an ounce of gas left. She had to drop down to one knee just to balance herself. Her head suddenly felt like a hollow rock—empty, but heavy as hell. Sounds began to pop in and out. But she could hear Skyler's footsteps approaching.

Get up. Get up off the ground.

She could have howled at herself for hours; it wouldn't have made a difference. No amount of self-imposed orders could change a thing. She was suddenly so weak, she could barely even hear her own thoughts.

Skyler knelt down next to her and raised her chin up with his finger to see her face. "Actually, Gaia," he said. "This right here. . . *this* was the plan." He smiled.

"What are you talking about?" she breathed. Even her own voice sounded far away—flying off into the dead air.

"I *know* you're not scared," he said. "I was counting on it."

She focused every ounce of her remaining energy into making a fist. If she could just make a fist for one last knockout blow to his repugnant face. . .

But her hand just sat there on the ground like a stone, barely propping her up on her knee. Her body would no longer listen.

"When. . . ?" she uttered. Forming words was becoming a herculean task. She was fading fast. Everything was fading. "When did you know. . . ?"

Skyler smiled. "Oh, there were a couple of weird moments in the past few days, but I couldn't quite be sure. That thing with the TV—that was a pretty big one. I mean, who just sits perfectly still when machine guns are suddenly going off in their house? Anyway, we had to be sure, so here was your test. Congratulations. You passed." He gave her a hard pat on the back and she fell like a leaf, collapsing flat on the ground. She stared at the sky, unable to move. It was all getting so dark, so far away. His voice was only an echo now.

"You look kind of tired," she heard him say, his voice dripping with irony. "We figured your treatment would wear off. We just couldn't be sure when it would happen. But it obviously did. So we were really counting on you *not* being afraid tonight. We wanted you to really fight your ass off. 'Cause we know what happens to you after a fight. Now you're so much more manageable."

They'd set a trap, and she'd fallen right into it. She couldn't predict their next move, and now she'd lost the game.

"It was a beautiful fight, Gaia," he added. "It really was. You should be proud. It's a great way to go out. Fighting. Like a hero."

Keep your eyes open. The only thing on earth you need to do right now is keep them open. If you close your eyes. . .

Skyler's face leaned into view above her, hovering under the dark black void. He was growing dimmer and dimmer, melding into the sky.

"I'll tell you a little secret," he whispered. "Just

between you and me. . . I'm going to miss you." He planted his hands on either side of her head, lowered his face down over hers, and gave her a long slow kiss, dipping his tongue between her lips.

And there was nothing she could do to stop him. She would have paid any price on earth to break his neck at that exact moment, but there was nothing she could do now. She couldn't even stay awake for her own ending.

"Good night, Gaia," he said.

Stay awake. You need to stay awake. She wouldn't close her eyes. She focused every ounce of her will on her eyes—to keep them open, to prolong her consciousness, to prolong her life for a few more seconds. It couldn't end like this. She *refused* to close her eyes.

But Skyler pressed his palm down on her eyelids. And he closed them for her.

Gaia's spine dropped to subzero temperatures. The name hovered in the air like poison gas. If she breathed it in, she would surely die.

the fatal blow

The Messenger

"THIS PROM SUCKS," MEGAN announced. "Who chose the music? The whole prom committee should be fired."

Ed didn't even try to hide his smile. This was one of the few true pleasures he could take in this evening: watching the FOHs having a positively lousy time.

"I know," Melanie agreed, leaning her face on her hand as she played with the ice in her empty glass. "Don't believe the hype."

Ed leaned back in his chair and surveyed the entire scene. He had to admit, had the circumstances been a little different, he probably could have had a good time at this thing. The truth was, the FOHs were flat-out wrong. The music was dead-on, and the venue was actually pretty cool. The Supper Club was like a big royal blue throwback to the 1940s, with a huge twenty-five-foot ceiling and a sweeping balcony. The place was downright elegant. The vibe was art deco, but there was funky music booming through the room, and Ed could appreciate the hip combination of the old and the new. He could definitely understand why most of the senior class seemed to be having a blast, whether they were going nuts on the dance floor or hanging at one of the round tables. He couldn't actually feel the pleasure of it himself, but he could

195

understand it from anyone else's point of view.

He scanned around his table, noting the wide variety of moods from person to person. Kai was next to him, bouncing her head to the music and sucking down a Diet Coke—she could pretty much have a good time no matter where she was. Liz Rodke and her date were next to her. Ed couldn't remember her date's name, or more likely, he was trying to block it due to the incredibly annoying way he had introduced himself. He'd announced his last name with this blue-blooded snob inflection—like his name was supposed to mean something to Ed, which it didn't. Which was precisely why Ed had happily forgotten it. Judging from the look on Liz's face, Ed thought she liked her date even less than he did. They'd hardly spoken a word to each other except for a few three-sentence exchanges about tennis.

Next to them were the FOHs. *Just* the FOHs. No dates. Apparently Rob Preston had managed to sneak in a bottle of Jack Daniels, and he and his football buddies had all disappeared to get ridiculously hammered *"one last time!"* as Rob had so subtly put it. The football boys were far more in love with each other than with their dates. Team first, Jack Daniels second, and their dates in a very distant third—thus were their priorities. At least until they'd gotten sufficiently plowed and came back to the girls for the official last booty call. Ed figured two out of the five guys *might* make it back for booty call, while the remainder would most likely be discovered in the bathroom at closing—their heads still hanging over the toilets—until the janitor, or possibly a chaperone, threw them out.

Once again Ed had to stop and take a certain pleasure in watching the FOHs' unbearably self-hyped evening go up in smoke. After all their endless bitchy speculation about a certain "other person's" prom date (Ed wouldn't think about that "other person's name), they'd basically ended up with no real dates of their own. Talk about poetic justice. Each one looked more miserable than the next, and it struck Ed as a most fitting end to their reign of bitchery. Although the true end to their reign was embodied in the girl sitting next to him on his right—Ed's one other true pleasure this evening.

Heather and Sam were having a genuinely good time, mostly due to the fact that Heather was as happy as Ed had seen her in a long while. Of everyone at their table Sam and Heather seemed to have the best understanding of this evening as a celebration. They had laughed and talked and even hit the dance floor, where Sam had kept her hand in his at all times just to avoid any potential head-on collisions. Ed had to admit, Sam had been a true gentleman.

Ed and Sam had already settled their "issues" (regarding the nameless person that Ed was very much *not* thinking about tonight—where the hell was she?), and so they could both relax to a certain degree and enjoy Heather's evening with her. Every couple of minutes another classmate would walk up to the table and ask Heather how she was feeling and tell her how thrilled they were for her recovery and how happy they were that she had graced the class one last time with her contagious smile and her beauty. Yes, they were mostly boys, which seemed to annoy the FOHs to no end, but still, Heather hadn't let it go to her head once. Her inner bitch seemed to have disappeared permanently, and it was a real joy for Ed to see. She'd accepted everyone's well-wishes with nothing but honest appreciation and humility. She reminded him so much of the old Heather—the sweet Heather that he'd fallen in love with freshman year, before she'd turned into a shallow, catty terror and made a certain someone's life hell for months (not that Ed was thinking about that certain someone, because he *wasn't*).

Indeed, Heather had been like a queen at this school—a queen who had somehow been corrupted, leading to a cruel, despotic reign that had lasted almost a year. And when she'd been exiled to Carverton, that had pretty much left Megan and the FOHs as a sort of horrible provisional government.

But Heather had come back tonight to take her rightful place as queen. The *good* queen. The Village

School had been returned to a benevolent monarchy on its last day, and Ed was happy to see it. The FOHs had finally been unseated. They had been rendered irrelevant—demoted back to second-tier popularity and they were pretty pissed about it, despite how much they loved Heather. Their reign had been brief, and they were feeling gypped. Not to mention being collectively dissed by their dates. Their resulting moods were so horrible that they chose to spew out `one last round of bitch bile` at the table and bring up the one topic Ed desperately did not want to discuss. They needed to feel superior one last time, so they brought up the name that Ed had been trying to forget all night.

"Um, you guys. . ." Megan was clearly addressing the entire table. She straightened her posture to make that clear. "Not that I *care*, but has anyone noticed who is notably missing from these tragic festivities?"

Ed winced and focused on his soda.

"Oh my God, yes," Melanie replied. It was the first time she had smiled for most of the night, but it was a sadistic kind of smile. "I *knew* it. I knew she would bag. Where the hell are Gaia and Jake?"

"Or Gaia and *Skyler*," Tammie added with a gossipy grin.

Out of his peripheral vision Ed could see that Sam was none too pleased to discuss the topic either. Liz looked even more troubled than Sam—probably at the mention of her brother.

"Maybe she couldn't find her gray sweatshirt." Laurie giggled. "And Jake and Skyler are helping her look for it." The ladies tittered.

"Or maybe she found her sweatshirt, but she couldn't find her cleats," Tammie added, upping the laughter quotient.

"Or JC Penney might have been out of black potato sack—"

"Meegs," Heather interrupted. "Mel. . ." There was an admonishing tone to Heather's voice that silenced all their laughter instantly.

"What?" Megan asked, shooting Heather a defiant glance back.

Heather gave her a long hard stare before speaking. "Nothing," she said politely. "It's just that I got over my Gaia jealousy a long time ago, and I think you should all probably do the same. It might give you a better sense of closure."

The FOHs went silent. Ed couldn't contain his smile at seeing them put in their place so handily by the benevolent queen.

"*Jealous?*" Megan finally huffed. "I'm not *jealous* of Gaia. That's ridic—"

"Meegs," Heather repeated calmly, "do you really want to go there?"

They seemed to share a silent conversation with

their eyes. A conversation that perhaps involved certain things Megan had said to Heather in confidence. Perhaps at a confessional slumber party, Ed figured, or maybe a particularly penetrating game of truth or dare.

"Whatever," Megan finally said, swallowing her word as she rolled her eyes.

"Yeah, whatever," Melanie echoed, stiffening her back. "The question still remains. . . Where are Gaia and Jake?"

Ed had been battling it like a warrior for the entire prom, but now Melanie had gone and weakened his goddamn resolve. He had very specifically *not* asked himself that question all damn night despite the fact that he had been asking himself that question all damn night. He didn't want to talk about it. And he desperately wanted to talk about it. Where was she?

"Maybe she had family stuff," Heather offered, shrugging. "It's none of our business. Maybe she just wasn't in the mood. Maybe she just thinks proms are silly. What's the big deal? If Gaia doesn't want to go, she doesn't have to go. Who knows, maybe she was just—"

"You guys," Liz interrupted. She was cringing slightly. "I don't know if I'm supposed to tell you all this. . . ."

All heads turned to Liz. Ed nearly got whiplash. "Tell us what?" he asked.

Liz looked down at her drink for a moment, and then she raised her head back up with a sad sort of regret in her eyes. "Well. . . I don't know about Jake. . . but I sort of heard that Gaia was leaving."

"What do you mean, 'leaving'?" Now Ed was asking all the questions in spite of himself.

"I mean. . . leaving town," Liz said. "I heard that she'd sort of had it with New York and that she was going to just skip graduation and prom altogether. I think she was going to Florida or something?"

The sudden silence at the table was like lead. Thick and heavy and impenetrable. Ed felt all the blood drain from his face, leaving his mouth slightly agape.

Heather was the first to finally break the silence. "Wait," she said, looking confused. "Wait, she's leaving. . . or she left?" Ed was glad she had asked. Because he very much wanted the same clarification. He just wasn't able to speak at this particular moment.

Liz clearly hated being the messenger on this one. Not to mention her own apparent melancholy, which seemed to be growing. "The sense I got. . . I think she's probably gone already."

Ed suddenly couldn't feel his fingers or his toes. Or his tongue, for that matter. In fact, he couldn't feel, period. His emotional mechanism had just overloaded so fast that he'd blown some kind of fuse. He could only sit there like a statue. Half the table had become statues. Ed and Sam and Heather and Liz. The FOHs didn't seem to know what to feel. Kai seemed to be silent out of some kind of respect for the other statues. And that left Liz's date.

"Who's Gi-yah?" he asked loudly. "What kind of a name is Gi-yah?" He looked around the table with a half smile of snobitude.

Ed excoriated him with his eyes. "*Gaia*," he snarled. "It's from Greek mythology. She was a goddess, she was the earth, she was life."

"Oh. . . 'Gaia,'" No-Name muttered. "I knew that." He retreated back into his chair.

Ed finally released the guy from his harsh stare. The deeply uncomfortable silence returned to the table. Until Sam finally broke it.

"Well. . . I guess. . ." Sam took a breath. "I guess I could understand that. Her leaving." His eyes looked empty as he said it.

"Yeah. . . ," Heather uttered, looking at the tablecloth. "I mean, I guess I could understand it, too." She turned to Sam. "After everything she's been through here, I don't know if I would want to stick around either."

"What has she been through?" Liz asked with concern.

Sam, Ed, and Heather all shared a series of awkward furtive glances.

"A lot," Sam breathed. He didn't seem quite sure

where to look when he said it. "She's been through a lot."

"Yeah." Heather sighed, slumping back in her chair. "I mean, if anyone deserves a vacation. . . it's Gaia Moore."

Sam coughed out a sad little blip of a laugh. "Amen," he mumbled.

The mood at the table grew more and more and somber.

"Um, *hello*," Tammie chimed in, shrugging. "The girl's not *dead*, you guys, she's just in Florida. What's with all the sad faces? Florida. . . ? The Sunshine State. . . ? She's lying in some hammock somewhere, eating oranges, with a Corona in her hand. What's the biggie?"

"Well, yeah. . . ," Kai offered tentatively. "I mean, we should just be happy for her then, right?" Leave it to Kai to look on the bright side. "I mean, I love Florida. Florida's beautiful this time of year. It's always beautiful there. I'm jealous."

"You know what? I am, too," Heather declared. "She's out there on some white sandy beach, just kicking back. If she can be happy there, then I think that's great. She deserves it."

"She does," Sam agreed. "She deserves it. All I ever wanted was for her to be happy."

Now all eyes seemed to be on Ed. As if they were waiting for him to concur. Like they needed him to make it unanimous that this was just great news. *Gaia has run off to sunny Florida! Hip hip hooray! Aren't you happy for her, Ed?*

But Ed wasn't there. He wasn't at that table anymore. His eyes were fixed on a dark corner of the Supper Club. That's where Ed was now. In that corner. His arms were firmly wrapped around Gaia's waist. Her arms were wrapped around the back of his neck. Her hair was falling into his face as she kissed him. He was breathing in her warm breath. She was pressing her body against his with more and more force. They had made it through every imaginable disaster together. They had made it to the finish line, and they were sharing one long, perfect kiss to prove it.

But then. . . piece by piece, Gaia's image began to disappear. Like a ghost. It wasn't just sad, it was disturbing somehow. It was ugly. She was fading away in chunks—first her head, and then her arms, then her torso, then her legs. She was being ripped apart and ripped away.

And then she was gone. And Ed was gone, too. The dark corner of the Supper Club was empty again. Just empty space.

That kiss wasn't going to happen. Never. And now Ed understood it as an absolute. And he had to accept it. He had to find some way to accept reality.

Aren't you happy for her, Ed?

Of course he wanted her to be happy. *Of course.*

That was the only thing he had ever cared about. He cared far more about her happiness than his own. That had been true since the moment he'd laid eyes on her angry scowl as she walked down the hallway of the Village School. He'd wanted to find a way to make that girl smile for a change.

But he couldn't just be happy for her. He couldn't. Maybe he wasn't as mature as Sam or Heather or anyone else at this table, but Gaia running off to Florida... it just felt totally *wrong* to him. It didn't feel real, it didn't feel right, it didn't feel true somehow. Could she really do that? Could she really just disappear without even saying goodbye to him?

Maybe she could. Maybe he didn't know Gaia Moore half as well as he thought he did. Maybe he never really had.

Either way, Ed had to accept it, whether it felt "wrong" or "real" or not. Gaia was gone. And if he knew anything about Gaia Moore, it was this:

Once she was gone, she was never coming back.

Certain things are meant
to be, and certain things are
not. I've always believed that.
Certain things are not about
probability or statistics,
they're just about facts. What
"is" and what "isn't."

Gaia and I were not meant to be.
I believe that now. I accept it.

What we had was so powerful at
first—our instant connection. More
powerful than anything I've ever
experienced. Maybe more powerful
than anything I ever *will* experience. From our first moment at that
chess table in the park, all the way
to that last moment together, right
before Loki's gunshot. . . every
moment between us was explosive.

But that's just the point.
Explosives combust. And then they
burn out, and then they fade
away. That was us. That is us. I
knew it from the moment I came
back—I just couldn't bring myself
to accept it until now.

Actually, I think that kind of
describes Gaia herself. All that

power, all that will, all that anger. . . She's combustible. She leaves this constant nuclear aftermath in her wake. But I guess that's finally over for her. I guess she was finally ready to let go—to burn out and fade away. Away from New York City, off to Florida, where she can finally relax; where she can finally put out the fire.

In a way, I think she said more to me by leaving than she ever could have said to my face. That's how I felt, sitting at that table in the Supper Club when I heard the news. I felt like, in her own way, she was sending me a final message.

Move on, Sam. For real this time. That's what I'm doing.

It took Gaia actually leaving town to drive it home, but I think maybe I can really start over now. I think maybe my normal life is finally beginning.

I will never love anyone as much as I loved Gaia Moore. Never.

But we never could have lived like that. All that explosive

power. It wouldn't have worked.
Because when all is said and done,
I don't think that's what life is
about—a big explosive high.

Life is about lasting. It's
about lasting for as long as we
possibly can. I've come back from
the dead once, and I never want
to try to do it again. Lasting.
That's it. That's all of it.

Gaia and I were simply not built
to last. But on my own. . . maybe
with some girl way down the line—
some girl who isn't quite so combustible. . . I think I could last
a pretty long time. I can only wish
the exact same for Gaia. Just a
long-lasting life. A life with
fewer explosions and less fire. I
think maybe she's found that on the
beach, by the ocean. All that water
to extinguish the flames. I don't
think I ever would have believed it
if she hadn't done it for herself,
but now I can actually see it. For
the first time I can actually see
Gaia Moore finding some peace. And
that makes me happier than she'll
ever know.

Life after death is just an illusion with a very simple explanation. And being the existentialist that I am, I'm more than happy to debunk the myth. I mean, I've heard all the ridiculous tales of people's "near-death experiences"—all the things they've seen while they were supposedly "on the other side"—the big white light, and the heavenly green field, and the ecstatic feeling of peace as they walked down that long tunnel.

But it's all a bunch of bull. It's all a purely biological phenomenon: when the blood stops flowing to your brain, you hallucinate. That's it. It's a proven fact. These people aren't seeing any "afterlife" during their precious two minutes of "death"—they're just plain old dreaming, basking in their little fantasies while the doctors are charging up the defibrillator.

I know that's what's happening to me right now. I know that I'm

GAIA

lying dead on the roof and that this sudden feeling of "waking up again" is nothing more than my dying hallucination. That's why this blinding white light is staring me in the face. That's why I can still hear Skyler talking. Jesus, what a tragic final hallucination. More Skyler Rodke.

Only there's another voice in my dying dream, too. And I've heard it before, I just can't quite place it. . . that German accent. . . . What is he saying?

"We need to finish up here. The procedure is going to take hours. . . ."

Dr. Ulrich. That's the other voice in my dream. The man who so generously "gave me fear." The man who will so generously be extracting all my internal organs once I'm—

Wait a minute.

I need to blink. I need to see past the white light. What if this isn't a hallucination? What if I'm not on the roof anymore?

Okay, either my dream is taking

a turn for the nightmarish, or I
know where I'm actually lying. I
can sense it. My body. . . it's
pinned down to a metal operating
table. That blinding white light
over my face. . . it's a surgical
light. I can hear Dr. Ulrich
standing at my side, talking
about "the procedure. . . ."

No, they wouldn't dare. They
couldn't. They couldn't do this
to me while I'm still alive. Even
the Rodkes aren't that sadistic.

Jesus, am I on an operating
table? Am I slowly dying as they
begin to pull me apart? I need
to blink away this blind spot. I
need to turn away from the
light. . . .

Death Row Criminal

GAIA FINALLY MANAGED TO TURN away from the blinding white light. The first thing she could see was her right arm. She followed the length of it until she saw her wrist. It was tied down with a thick, buckled leather strap, and that strap was tied securely to the bed. *That's* what she was lying on. Not an operating table, not the roof of Skyler's building. . . but a bed. And she was strapped to it. Both arms. Both legs.

She slammed her eyes shut again just for one moment—just to curse her entire existence. *Restraints.* She swore to herself on all that was holy that no matter *what,* no matter what was going on right now, whether she was going to live for another sixty years or another sixty seconds... this was the last time she would ever awaken in restraints.

"Karl. . ." She could hear Skyler's voice above her. "Karl, I think she's coming to."

She ripped open her eyes again, squinting to dodge that glaring white light. She realized now that it wasn't a surgical light, but simply the lamp over Skyler's bed, hanging much too close to her face.

She was back in Skyler's apartment. She could still see the night through the panes of his bedroom window. How much time had passed since the roof?

"What the hell is this?" Gaia croaked, trying to spot Skyler's sickening face through her squinting eyes.

"Shhh." Skyler placed his finger to his lips. "I think you want to go back to sleep." He looked at Ulrich across the bed. "Couldn't we have put her out for this?"

"We don't have time to wait for the anesthetic," Ulrich replied with his thick German accent. He sounded like a Nazi in every sense of the word. "I didn't expect her to wake so soon."

Gaia flipped her head back to Ulrich and tried to speak with something stronger than a hoarse whisper. "What are you doing to me?" she mumbled. "What the hell are you—?"

"Ms. Moore, *please*," Ulrich interrupted. "Please try to be still, and this can all go much more quickly. I'm sorry you had to witness this, but I had hoped you would stay unconscious for much—"

"You're *sorry?*" She strained to wake the muscles in her face. "If you're so sorry, then take these *off*." She tugged at her restraints.

"I'm afraid I can't do that. That would make this entirely too difficult. But I promise you it won't be long now. I am working as quickly as I can." He turned back to Skyler. "Bring the other drip over and we'll begin. This is difficult to do with her awake." Ulrich averted his eyes and rolled some kind of metal pole into view next to the bed. Skyler was rolling one over from the other side.

214

No, not a pole, a "drip." An intravenous drip. An IV. . .

Gaia understood. She knew what they were going to do to her. She knew what these two intravenous drips were for. One for each arm. It was Ulrich's very own little "suicide machine." They weren't going to rip out her insides while she was still alive; they were going to "put her down" first. There were no psycho orderlies with syringes—that had just been a fake out—but this. . . this was the real thing. The *real* lethal injection. Gaia was about to be euthanized. Just like they did it on death row. She'd awoken just in time to witness her own death.

She turned back to Skyler as reality began to sink in. "Why didn't you just shoot me?" she uttered. "You could have started the autopsy hours ago."

Skyler's eyes widened with surprise. But then a slow smile of epiphany began to creep up on his face. "*Man,* you're good. You are really good. You read my e-mail, didn't you? That whole Jake e-mail thing was total bull, wasn't it? You just wanted my password so you could hack into my e-mail. Gaia, I am really impressed."

Gaia stared at his patronizing smile. "Screw you." She tried again to send a jolt of energy to her limbs, but it was utterly pointless.

Skyler laughed, although Gaia was by no means

joking. He leaned down by her side with that same look of admiration that she was beginning to think wasn't even fake. "There is no way we would shoot you," he said. "You think we would fire a bullet through this perfect body? We need everything pristine. Gaia, you are this perfect thing; you're this genetic masterpiece—we need every single organ, every vein, every artery intact. . . ."

"All right, enough," Ulrich announced. "We're about ready here. Now, you're sure you've covered all the bases for her disappearance? I'm not going to have your father shouting at me about—"

"It's taken care of," Skyler assured him, standing back up. "I planted the whole story with Liz. She thinks Gaia's leaving town and heading down to Florida to 'get lost.' I guarantee you she'll pass it on to the whole school by the end of tonight. The girl can't keep a secret." He turned back to Gaia. "By the way, if it means anything to you, Liz doesn't know a thing about any of this. Like I said. . . can't keep a secret."

Actually, it meant a lot. More than Gaia even thought it would mean. It was good to know that she hadn't misplaced *every* ounce of her trust in this life. It gave her another bolt of energy to challenge those restraints, which led to nothing but more burning pink skin on her wrists and ankles.

"Let's begin, then," Ulrich said. "I want to get this over with."

Her life, he meant. He wanted to get her life over with. Ulrich leaned down to her with the IV needle in his hand, and he began to tap her arm for the vein.

Jesus Christ. This was how she was going to die. Euthanized like a death row criminal. She almost wished she hadn't woken up. Because there was absolutely nothing she could do. No amount of fighting spirit could change anything. Her body was strapped so tightly to that bed, she could hardly move a muscle. Even if she could, she was too weak to make a dent in those leather straps.

Ulrich inserted the needle into her arm, and then he moved around to the other side of the bed to insert the second. Gaia searched her brain desperately for some answer, some brilliant scheme, but there was nothing. Literally no room to maneuver.

He inserted the needle into her other arm, and then he moved back around the bed to press the switch and end her life.

Maybe there is an afterlife, she told herself. *And I've just been too cynical to believe it.*

Or maybe she just needed to believe that, in this last moment. Maybe she needed to believe a lot of things that she had never believed before.

It could be. It could be just like what all those people said: A warm white light. A green field. Blue skies and crystal blue water. . . Wait a minute! What the hell is the matter with you? You sound like you've given up already. Make your body move. Wake it up! You have to fight this. You have to fight this tooth and nail. This is your life here. This is the end of it. The real end. Somehow, some way, you need—

But she never got to finish that thought. It was drowned out completely by the sudden blast of gunfire that tunneled through the hallway like fireworks.

And this time it wasn't the TV.

"YOU! DOWN ON THE GROUND. NOW!"

Gaia's eyes snapped open to see Loki, Jake, and Chris piling into Skyler's bedroom. Loki had both hands clamped securely to his gun, and he was pointing it at Ulrich. He'd already shot out the lock of the front door and kicked it down, and he was clearly aiming to shoot again.

Tragic Futility

It was all suddenly chaos. All these men shouting at the same time. Loki was barking out orders; Ulrich and Skyler were desperately insisting that he put down the gun; Chris and Skyler were hollering at each other; Jake was calling out to Gaia to see if she was okay. . . . She could hardly separate one man's shouts from the others.

"I'm okay," she uttered. "I am." But her weak-voiced assurances were no match for the din of male voices in the room.

"You don't need to shoot!" Ulrich bellowed. "Please." He placed his hands over his head.

"I said the floor!" Loki hollered. "Down on the floor, now!" He pushed the gun into Ulrich's head, and Ulrich followed orders. "Jake, undo those restraints."

"Right," Jake said. He rushed to the bed and finally relieved the aching pressure from Gaia's wrists and ankles. He took the IV needles out of her arm. Then he knelt at her bedside as she tried to rub the feeling back into her wrists. "Are you okay?"

Gaia finally got a good look at Jake's face, and her mouth dropped open in horror. He looked like he'd taken the beating of his life. He was covered in dark red bruises, and his hand was wrapped with a thick bandage. "Jesus, what happened to you?" she uttered.

"Don't worry about it," he said, gripping her hand and smiling. "It doesn't matter now."

She could tell he wanted to say more, but Skyler was screaming so loudly from behind him, she couldn't have heard him. Skyler was staring at his brother with the purest scorn.

"God*damn* it, Chris, you freaking screwup! What the hell have you done?"

"What are *you* doing?" Chris shot back. "What the hell were you going to do to her?"

"I *knew* it," Skyler complained. "I *knew* you would find some way to screw this up. I *told* Dad, keep the dunce out of this—"

"Enough!" Loki barked, pointing the gun at Skyler. But Skyler's eyes were fixed on his brother's.

"You are so pathetic, Chris, you know that? You are so goddamn useless."

"Shut your mouth!" Chris hollered. "I beat you both, and you know it."

"*Beat* us? You just put us all in *jail*, Chris. *All of us.* If you think you're not going with us, then you're an even bigger idiot than I thought you were. This is what we get for putting up with your pathetic pansy ass. This is what we get. God, you are *so* hopeless. . . ." Skyler began to laugh with `tragic futility`. "Hey, does anybody here want a gay brother? Because we are so done with him."

"I said, *enough*," Loki ordered.

"Anyone?" Skyler laughed harder. "Gaia? Jake? No? Well, I'm sure they'll want you in prison, Chris. I'm sure you'll have a ball. I'm sure you'll be somebody's bitch by the end of the first day—"

"Shut your goddamn *mouth!*" Chris howled.

No one expected it. No one expected him to reach for Loki's gun. It all happened so fast, before anyone could really think.

Chris barreled into Loki, taking him by complete surprise, and he snatched the gun from his hand. He thrust it in Skyler's direction, his eyes blazing with anger, and he began to fire off shot after wild shot. The window shattered into jagged pieces, holes exploded in every book, every picture frame. Skyler was knocked back against the wall as two shots clipped his right arm. Loki reached for Chris. Gaia pushed off from the bed to knock him down.

Jake was a step of ahead of her. He leapt up from the floor and flew for Chris's torso. . . .

But two gaping bullet holes erupted in Jake's chest.

A rare sound fell from Gaia's mouth. A scream. Loud, and deep, and quick. Jake fell flat at Chris's feet as blood began to pour from his wounds.

All Gaia had left were her reflexes. She shot across the room and kicked the gun from Chris's hand. It dropped to the floor as Loki tackled him to the ground. Gaia turned back for the gun and realized that it had dropped right in front of Ulrich. He snatched it up from the floor and began to rise, and Gaia knew at that moment that she was prepared to kill him. There would be no remorse. She smacked the gun from his hands with a sweeping roundhouse kick, and then she riddled his body with a punishing combination of kicks and punches until his face was covered with blood. She grabbed his head with an animal instinct, ready to snap his neck. . . .

But the booming voice from the hallway stopped her just short of murder.

"CIA!" the voice bellowed.

The sound of stampeding feet echoed through the hallway as a pack of black-suited agents suddenly stormed the bedroom. One of them pulled Ulrich immediately from her grip, tugging his hands behind his back and cuffing him.

"Ms. Moore? Are you all right?" The agent looked hard at her for some kind of acknowledgment. "It's over," he assured her. "It's all over."

Gaia didn't even look at him. She shoved him out of the way and dropped down next to Jake, grabbing hold of his hand.

"Jake?" She searched his eyes desperately. He was taking shallow, labored breaths. His body wasn't moving. Only his eyes. His eyes turned to hers, and she could see him trying to forge a reassuring smile with his lips as he stared at her. The entire front of his shirt was drenched in blood.

"We need an ambulance here!" Her voice cracked as she called out. "Somebody call nine-one-one. . . ."

She felt Jake's grip beginning to loosen in her hand. The remnants of the smile were fading from his face.

"Stay with me, Jake," she ordered. "Listen to me. Keep your eyes open. You stay with me."

He forced his eyes open again and squeezed her hand. But she was losing him. She could feel it. She could see it in his shallow breaths and his dilating pupils. She was losing him.

JAKE STOPPED BREATHING. AND SO

Detached

did Gaia. Gaia wasn't even sure what was keeping her from falling onto the floor right next to him. She couldn't feel her body anymore. She couldn't even feel his hand, still lying in hers, limp and without a pulse. She knew there were tears pouring from her eyes, but she wasn't crying. She wasn't there anymore. She was no longer in that room.

None of this was real. It was that simple. It was the only possible explanation for this uninhabitable moment. Jake wasn't lying on the floor. Agents weren't pronouncing him dead and prying his hand from her tight grip, lifting his body off the ground, and carrying it slowly down the hallway. Ulrich and Chris weren't being read their rights and escorted out of the room. Skyler wasn't having his bloody arm tugged brutally behind his back and cuffed. He wasn't growling about the pain as nobody listened.

It simply wasn't possible. Her curse couldn't have taken another victim. It had to be a dream. Loki was sitting next to her on the floor with tears in his eyes. That couldn't be real. Because he never cried.

He was kneeling beside her, watching as the agents carried Jake's body down the hall. "I am so sorry," he breathed. She couldn't tell if he was talking to her or to Jake. He turned and spoke to her vacant profile as her eyes stayed fixed on the empty hallway. "This never should have happened," he said. "None of this."

"It's not happening," she replied in a detached monotone, shaking her head slowly. "None of this is happening."

"Gaia—"

"*Shhh.*" She shut her eyes and wrapped herself deeper in a thick, impenetrable blanket of denial. She would just stay under the blanket until this moment went away—until Jake walked back through that door, alive and smiling, with those ungodly bruises erased from his face. He would walk back down the hallway and kneel down next to her, and she would kiss his handsome, clean-shaven face and thank him for barging through Skyler's bedroom doorway when he did—for saving her life, for leaping fearlessly from the ground to disarm Chris. She would thank him for everything, and then she would forgive him. For falling under Loki's spell and for not believing in her. After all, he had been right. She *had* needed him in that final moment. If he had listened to her, then she wouldn't be alive right now.

But Jake would have been. And that had been her point. It had been her point all along. They had both been right and they had both been wrong. But only one of them was gone now, and as far as she was concerned. . . it was the wrong one. But no, *no*. He was coming back. He'd be coming back in just a second. Just one more second. . .

The cold wet tears sealed her eyelashes shut. When she felt Loki's hand take hers, she didn't even pull away. That was how numb she was.

"Listen to me," he said. "Gaia, please. I am so, so sorry. I never—"

"You did this!" she screamed. It had come roaring from out of nowhere. A wave of primitive anger. It sprang from deep in her chest like a hundred-year-old water pipe that had finally burst. Her eyes were wide open, shooting daggers through Loki, ripping the skin from his face. "*You* brought him into this. . . . *You*. . ."

"I know," he said. His voice quavered as another tear fell from his eye. "I know that. I—"

"This is *your* fault!"

"I know that. . . ." It seemed to be all he could say.

Her anger dropped away just as quickly as it had appeared. It was like a death spasm, an aftershock. She had spewed out the last ounce of her strength, and now she was even weaker than before—sapped of all her remaining force. Her well of feelings had gone bone-dry. Even the tears had stopped. She could feel the air passing through her hollow frame.

"Gaia, I know what I've done," he said. "And I will never be forgiven for it. Not for any of it, not by anyone. And I never should be. But I know. . . you will survive this. You need to understand that. That's the only thing that matters now—that you will survive all

225

of it. You're not like me. You haven't gone cold, you haven't given in to spite, you haven't lost faith. You survive. You survive everything. And you'll survive this too—"

"Shut up!" she snapped. "Stop talking."

"I'm sorry." He went silent. But he wouldn't stop staring at her. She would have done something to him—something violent—but she didn't have it in her anymore. She needed all her remaining energy to maintain her denial. She couldn't allow one more crack in her emotional armor. One more crack and there would be a chain reaction of geological proportions—volcanic fissures would spread across her frozen-over heart like wildfire and she would simply combust; she would be lying in molten pieces on the ground.

"If they had just gotten here sooner," she breathed, staring down at the pool of blood on the floor. "If they had gotten here one minute sooner, he'd still be—"

Gaia cut herself off. It had all happened so fast, she hadn't even had a chance to think about it. She was going to call the Agency. That had been the plan. Once the Rodkes made their move, she had planned to take them down and then call in the agents. But she'd never gotten the chance. So then who. . . ?

"Who called the Agency?" she asked herself. She hadn't even meant to say it out loud.

"I did," Loki replied.

Gaia's eyes widened in spite of herself. She couldn't even stop herself from turning back to his eyes with sheer disbelief. "You called them...?"

Loki looked grateful just to have her attention again. "I called them," he confirmed. "Gaia, this has to end. All of it, all the violence in your life, it has to stop. That's the key to your survival, and that's all I care about now. You can't survive with all these enemies hovering around you. Not just the Rodkes, but *all* of your enemies—all the people who have tried to hurt you...

"*I* have to stop," he declared. "I can't be your enemy anymore. I won't. I'll never understand how it happens, I'll never understand why it happens, but I refuse to let it happen again."

Gaia couldn't speak. If she attempted even one word, she was sure that would begin the internal combustion process.

"I need to repent," he uttered quietly. "For so many crimes. More than I can even list. I need to repent for the attempted murder of your father and Sam Moon... for the murder of Josh Kendall... and Mary Moss." Loki glanced at her. I won't be bothering you for a while. I need to disappear and repent."

Gaia's spine dropped to subzero temperatures. The name hovered in the air like poison gas. If she breathed it in, she would surely die. But she wasn't breathing. Her lungs and her heart seemed to cease functioning. She was unable to blink or swallow. All she could do was stare at Loki's darkly remorse-ful eyes as he nodded to confirm it.

Mary? Loki killed Mary? Gaia had always thought it was Mary's dealer, Skizz. She had never thought anything else, ever. She had barely even *met* her uncle then—she hadn't even known he existed. But when he confessed it, she knew it was true. He had destroyed her life before she even knew him. He had stabbed Mary Moss in cold blood, and Gaia had watched it happen. A seventeen-year-old girl. Gaia's best friend in the world.

Now Gaia felt like the one who had been stabbed in the heart. Her eyes began to sting with pain and she could no longer close them. She watched in frozen silence as Loki touched her shoulder with one last glance of deep contrition. He offered more apologies, but she couldn't even hear them. It was like she was watching him speak with the sound turned off. He rose up off the floor, kissed her cheek, and then backed away from her slowly, backing farther and farther down the hallway... and then vanishing from sight.

Gaia still couldn't move. She could barely even focus her thoughts on Loki. She was cursed to keep seeing those images rerun through her head—playing, and rewinding, and then playing again, over and over. Images of blood-soaked shirts. Mary's and Jake's. So much blood pouring out of their chests, right where their hearts should have been. Images of Gaia clinging to each one of them as they bled—knowing that she was the one and only reason that these remarkable people had endured so much pain... and lost their lives before they'd even started.

That was it. That was all she could take. Loki's confession was the fatal blow to her emotional armor, and she could feel it happening now. She could practically see the cracks spreading out in dark black branches all over her skin. She could practically feel her heart ripping slowly at the seams, crumbling down to the pit of her stomach. The truth was pouring in through all the cracks, flooding her to the gills: Jake wasn't coming back through that hallway. He was never coming back again.

No, she couldn't stay in this moment. If she lived in this moment for one more second, she would surely end up in pieces on the ground. Pieces too small to ever be put back together.

Without another thought, she shot up off the floor and bolted down the hallway, leaping the fallen door and hurling herself down the stairs in huge leaps. She tried to erase Loki entirely from her memory with every step, believing for the very first time that she would never see him again.

She crashed through the doorway of Skyler's building and took off down the street. She had to run faster and harder than she had ever run before. She had to outrun this moment. If she let it catch up with her, she would be blown to bits.

Trying to outrun her past was like trying to outrun

west village moses

a tidal wave or a flood of biblical proportions.

I have to thank God for the remnants of my sanity. And by "God," I mean Chris Rodke. Because without him I'm not sure I would have seen it. I'm not sure I would have come to terms with the simple fact:

I am not sane. I have not been sane for a very long time. Not since I was a young man not much older than Chris.

I know now why I was so anxious to kill that boy. It was not just that he was another painful reminder of the offspring I will never have. It ran much deeper than that. Looking at Chris was like looking in a mirror. And I was sickened by what I saw.

I saw a boy who despised his favored brother with all of his heart. A boy who felt so invisible, so ineffectual, so shunned by the family he loved that he wanted to see them hurt. He wanted to see them dead. He wanted to prove his power, and his inferiority complex grew like a cancer

into a tragic God complex. It is
amazing the things we cannot see
in ourselves that are so glar-
ingly obvious in others.

It had all sounded so laughable to me. A boy referring to
himself as "God," giving himself
this ludicrously bloated identity
to mask some shattered adolescent
ego. It sounded truly pathetic.
Until I realized. . . that boy
was me. *Pathetic*. A man who calls
himself "Loki," the Norse god of
the underworld. How small I must
have felt on that fateful day in
1990 when I announced my own
deification. How very small. . .

There were really two mirrors
looking back at me in that limousine. Two young men. . . two
images of my tragic schizoid
past. Jake, God rest his soul,
reminded me so much of a young
Green Beret named Oliver Moore.
More than I think I even understood. His unyielding strength
and independence and intelligence, his uncommon command of
the martial arts at such a young

age, his naive ambition to trans-
form himself into some kind of
all-American "superspy."

And Chris Rodke reminded me so
much of a demented young agent
named Oliver. Pride as a disease.
Pride turned into megalomania and
envy and a vengeful killer
instinct. An insatiable need for
control.

One boy was the man I could
have been. . . and one was the
man I had become—a man who needs
to repair his ravaged psyche and
repent for his sins. It wasn't
just Chris I wanted to murder. It
was that mirror image. I wanted
to shoot enough holes in that
mirror to make me disappear.

But only I can make me disappear. The devil in me, that is. I
have to seek help. I have to heal
myself. I can't even imagine how
many lucky future souls have been
spared now that Chris Rodke has
been put away. I only wish I
could say the same for all the
poor souls who have crossed my
path for the last twenty years.

They have not been so lucky. And
I will never be forgiven.

   I am so sorry, Jake. You will
never know how deeply sorry I am
for bringing you into my ugly
world. You are the one who should
have been—the one who should have
had a future, just as Oliver
Moore should have been the man I
am today, instead of the sick
thing that I have become.

   But you were right, Jake. You
were right. We wanted the same
thing. All we wanted was to see
Gaia safe and sound—finally out
of harm's way. And with the
Agency picking up Robert Rodke at
his office and me starting down
the path to righteousness. . . I
think we've done it. I think
we've finally given Gaia the
future that she deserves. She
deserves what you and I have
given her, Jake. She deserves to
be free.

If I could actually stop for a
moment. . .

If I could allow myself time
to think, then this is what I'd
be thinking:

I loved you, Jake. I did. More
than I could admit, more than I
could face, more than I could
deal with. I know I lost faith in
you somehow. I felt you giving
over to Loki and I didn't know
how to stop you. I didn't know
how to save you from it. But I
think I know now why you did it.
I think I know why you fell under
his spell. You just wanted the
same thing I've wanted since I
was six years old. . . .

To be a hero.

You thought my uncle was some
kind of hero. You thought you
were following in his footsteps.
You just wanted to *save* people.
And you did, Jake. You saved me.

I wish to God that you'd been
spared my curse. The curse of
Gaia Moore. If anyone on this
earth was a match for it, it was

you. You have more force in you,
more strength, more power than
anyone I've ever—

No. Not *have*. *Had*. You had
more force in you. Past tense
now. All that force was ripped
away. Because of me. And I'm not
sure I can live with that. I'm
not exactly sure how I'll ever
move forward now that I've let
fate take you away. You always
fought for me, Jake. And you
fought side by side *with* me. No
man has ever done that the way
you did. And I don't think I'll
ever let another man try. I'll
never fight side by side with
another man. I'm not even sure
I'll ever let another man into my
life at all. I don't think I
could take the pain of losing
him. Not after you, Jake. Not
after you died just to save my
life.

I did love you, Jake. I honestly did.

No. I *do*. I do love you.
Present tense.

But I can't think about it

now. I'm sorry, but I can't. Remember? This is all what I'd be thinking *if* I could stop for a moment. *If* I could allow myself time to think. And I can't. I can't stop and I can't think. To put it in no uncertain terms: if I stop. . . I think I'll die.

GAIA COULD FEEL THE CITY CRUMBLING
behind her with every step. Trying
to outrun her past was like trying
to outrun a tidal wave or a flood **A Flood**
of biblical proportions. Like a
mountain of violent water nipping at her back,
looming ominously close to crashing
down over her head and swallowing her
whole. She had never even realized how far she
could run if she truly believed her life depended on it.
Her feet felt like raw meat, and her entire body was
sheened with a thick layer of sweat, but she had run
with every ounce of her will for more than a hundred
blocks.

She had sprinted past the empty Village School,
past the empty Niven town house on Perry Street, past
Gray's Papaya, past at least ten Krispy Kremes. She
could imagine them being ripped from their founda-
tions by the wave, being smashed to pieces like cheap
insignificant toys, crashing into each other, turning
into nothing but broken chunks that threatened to
crush her from behind. She had sprinted through
Washington Square Park, where the wave had pried
the Arc de Triomphe from the ground and all the
stone chess tables. It was all crumbling down.

Her mother's body was in the wave, along with
Mary's and Ella's and George's and now Jake's. Their
corpses were being thrown violently from side to side,

like toy dolls stuck in the undertow. And Gaia felt like she would be next.

Or maybe she *wanted* to be next. Maybe she felt like she deserved it. Of course she deserved it. She was the reason for all their deaths—maybe even her mother's in a way. Who knew? Maybe if her parents hadn't had a daughter, Loki wouldn't have gotten so murderously jealous? Maybe all the carnage in Gaia's wake never would have even started? Maybe the entire world would have been spared the curse of Gaia Moore.

I am so sorry, Jake. You have no idea. You will never know. Never.

Memories of Jake were flooding her head. Now he had been sucked into the wave—just another body in the collective Gaia wreckage careening toward her. She flashed back to their days in the park, the fights they had fought together, the fights they'd had with each other. . . . The flashbacks were getting stirred into the tragic soup, along with her memories of Mary—their night at the Thanksgiving floats and those long, endless walks where they'd laugh and laugh about nothing.

But all those thoughts only made her run faster. She couldn't face any of it. She couldn't allow herself to stand still. If she truly considered how much she would miss Jake, she was doomed. If she thought for another minute about Mary, she was done for. She could *not* allow herself to go back in time anymore or that wave would eat her alive. It would be the end of what little sanity she had left. It would finally be time to toss her in that padded cell and throw away the key. For *real* this time.

If she could just make it all disappear. If she could just pound her staff down in the middle of Bleeker Street, like a West Village Moses, and part that bloody sea of dead souls and demolished buildings—watch it pour onto either side of the street, just like in the Charlton Heston movie, leaving her on a dry, narrow path that was safe for her to walk through. There had to be some way to make it disappear. All of it. *She* had to disappear. . . .

And then, quite suddenly, she stopped running. She stopped right smack in the middle of Houston Street and doubled over, grasping her thighs as she stared at the gutter and heaved for breath. She had just had a revelation.

If I could disappear. . .

The irony was almost too much to bear.

The Rodkes had been planning her disappearance for weeks. They had already laid all the groundwork. They had said all her goodbyes. They had carved out that dry, narrow path she'd been yearning for. The path to the promised land—also known as *somewhere else.*

To escape. To leave it all behind and never look back. That was the answer.

Skyler Rodke had inadvertently given her this tremendous gift. The devil had somehow shown her the path *out* of hell by mistake. He had already put a period on this part of her life. And Gaia was going to use it. She could make his fake story true—minus, of course, the Florida part. She could leave New York City and start an entirely new life in a place that had stars at night. A place where nobody knew her name or her genetic makeup. A place where her past wouldn't haunt her to death.

A new place. That was it. It was time for a new place.

And suddenly that tidal wave didn't seem so ominous anymore. She had simply been looking at it wrong. She'd been looking back at the water with apocalypse-colored glasses, filling it with the properties of death and destruction. But she had her symbols wrong.

Waves and waters and oceans. . . The last time she checked, they didn't represent death. They represented *rebirth*. Baptisms and beginnings, not endings. The wave wasn't going to swallow her up in her past. It was going to wash her past away.

Gaia took a deep breath and turned around. She could see it now. She could see it right up Sixth Avenue. Not blood and death and disaster. She could see the way out. And it was time to start running.

"GOD, WHERE DO YOU THINK WE'LL
all be five years from now? Ed. . . ?"

"Huh?" Ed wasn't listening. He
had stopped listening to everything
about two hours ago. The entire
world had drifted about ten feet
away. It had all turned into a very
bad drive-in movie, barely visible,
hard to hear, and filled with pointless, cheesy melodrama.

**Tearfu
Good
Night**

Half the class was standing on the
street outside the Supper Club like a pack of seals
barking. The prom was over, but they were trying to
drag it out for as long as they possibly could, which
was particularly ridiculous given that they would all
just end up at the same after party at Allison Rovitz's.
Still, they were trying to milk this moment for
all it was worth, whining their drunken good
nights—each one more clichéd than the last. "I'll miss
you *so much* after graduation." "I love you." "I never
told you this, but I always loved you." "I never told you
this, but I loved you, and then I hated you, and then I
loved you again." "I never told you this, but I always
wanted to have sex with you. . . . Are you drunk?"

Even Kai had fallen prey to the sentimental disease.
She had caught the "where will we all be in five years?"
bug that was floating through the crowd. So Ed pretended not to hear her.

Where would he be in five years? He honestly didn't care. What he cared about was now and how dismally depressing now had turned out to be. The truth was, he was lying his ass off to himself again. He didn't really think the tearful good nights were so cheesy. Proms were made for tearful good nights. It was just that there was only one tearful good night he'd wanted—only one that would have truly meant something to him. And it wasn't going to happen.

Somehow that fact seemed to nullify so much of his past. It cast this hideous pall over his entire relationship with Gaia Moore. He could have lived without the kiss. He had already learned how to live without her kiss. But the friendship. . . that was something else. That had been the foundation for everything. And if Gaia thought their friendship wasn't even worthy of one last goodbye, then Ed couldn't help but think that he'd projected a great deal onto what they had. All those milk shakes. . . all those bagels and Froot Loops and chili dogs at Gray's. From that first exchange in the hall to the most amazing night of his life and every day and night in between. . . if he couldn't look back on the two of them as soul mates, then he would have to pretty much give up on the concept of "soul mate" altogether. If he and Gaia weren't it, then there was clearly no such thing. And what he wanted most now was not to discuss where he would be in five years. What he wanted was to go home and lie down in his tux and try to dial down his general expectations of the world in preparation for college.

"Ed, are you there?" Kai sighed.

Ed turned to her with an apologetic glance. He sure as hell hoped Kai found better friends than him out there in the world because he'd done a pretty lousy job of it. And tonight would be no exception.

"Hey," he said, desperately hoping not to hurt her feelings. "Do you think you'd be cool heading to the after thing solo? I think I'm getting a little sick."

Kai looked into his eyes, and then she smiled forgivingly. "Sure," she said. "I understand." He knew she understood far more than she was saying, and they shared one last hug.

"Thanks," he said. "You looked absolutely stunning tonight. I'm sorry if I was—"

"You weren't." She grinned. "You were a great date."

"No, I wasn't." He smiled. "You deserved better."

"Well. . . maybe in five years? Dinner at the Supper Club?"

"Absolutely. Or maybe next week?"

"Even better," she said.

He kissed Kai on the cheek and they said their last goodbyes, and then he stepped over to Heather and Sam and gave them his sick story. They of course immediately understood the code. Heather threw her arms around him and gave him a long and powerful hug.

"I love you, Ed. I honestly do."

"I love you, too," he replied with his mouth muffled in her hair.

She gripped his shoulders and gave him one last looking over. "She'll be okay, Ed. I know she will."

"I know," Ed said.

"Call me tomorrow?"

"I will."

Ed turned to Sam and gave him a firm handshake. Their eyes locked with some kind of understanding. Something about this night and hearing the news of Gaia's departure had left them with a new mutual respect. "Keep a good watch on her tonight," Ed said, referring to Heather. "No ice hockey or anything."

Heather slapped Ed playfully on the arm.

"Will do," Sam said.

"Okay. . . good night. You two were great tonight."

They smiled graciously. And with that, Ed turned around and began his long walk home with his hands buried deep in his tuxedo pockets. The sound of the crowd drifted off behind him, and he was supremely conscious of walking away from his past and trying to focus on his future. He didn't do a very good job of it, though. By the fifth building from the club all he could really think about was his past. No amount of rationalization could truly take his mind off thoughts of what should have been.

Move on, Ed. Just keep moving. It's just a goodbye. You'll survive it. You'll—

But Ed never finished that thought. He never had the chance. It was ripped away by brute force. By the last nightmare of the evening. The one thing he always dreaded in the city but still never expected. The thing no one in New York ever expects despite the fact that they're always just waiting for it to happen. . .

A late-night mugging in a garbage-filled alley on Forty-seventh Street.

Two hands reached out from a dark narrow alley and slammed up against his back, tugging him violently off the street and into the shadow. Ed just couldn't believe it.

In that one split second, before his body was snapped back into the alley like a rag doll, he was completely crushed by a wave of bitter disbelief—by the cold, merciless irony that could only exist in New York.

This can't be happening, he thought. *Not tonight. I've already lost everything tonight. I can't possibly be losing my money and my life, too.*

But it was happening. And there was nothing he could do to stop it. The worst night of his life was going to end with an armed robbery and a shot in the head.

"I don't *have* any money," Ed spat. "I just came from. . ."

But his voice suddenly trailed off into silence. Because Ed had finally turned to face down the mugger in the alley. And the mugger. . . wasn't a mugger at all.

SHE DIDN'T EVEN SPEAK AT FIRST.

Faith

Nor did Ed. He could only stand and stare at the half of her perfect face that he could see, dimly lit by the fluorescent outdoor lights of the Korean deli on the corner. The sound of passing traffic echoed off the narrow brick walls of the alley. He wasn't sure how to fill the noisy silence. He wasn't sure what to say. He was still in a mild state of shock at the sight of her.

He couldn't even read the half of her expression that he could see. She was neither happy nor sad. She looked a bit like she'd been to hell and back, but she always looked that way. After a series of lightning-quick half thoughts and a batch of deeply overwhelming emotions, Ed finally spoke one of the dumbest half thoughts of them all.

"You're. . . not in Florida."

"No," Gaia said, keeping her eyes fixed on his.

"No," he repeated. She apparently didn't plan to say much. "You're. . . leaving for Florida?"

"No," she replied. "But I am leaving."

"Oh." Ed's heart began to sink again.

"Ed, I just. . ."

The sound of a group of laughing seniors came from down the block. Gaia glanced at the street, and then she grabbed Ed's lapel, pulling him deeper into the alley. The light was even dimmer this far in, but at least there was a bit more quiet.

"Are you okay?" he asked. "Gaia, what's going on?"

"I am okay," she said, rather oddly. "Right now. Right now I am okay."

Ed stepped closer to her, and now he could see that her hair was soaking wet with sweat, as were her T-shirt and her jeans. "Hey. . . what happened to you? Did you just run a marathon instead of attending your senior prom?"

"You could say that. Sort of."

Ed listened more closely to her voice, and suddenly he understood. It hit him hard in the center of his chest. He had finally heard her speak enough words to make sense of her hesitance and her strange inflections. He knew this voice of hers. This careful measured monotone. It was the voice Gaia used when she was trying not to cry.

He took a step closer so that they were nearly nose to nose, and he forgot about every stupid negative thought he'd had this evening and most of the week and most of the weeks before that. He dropped it all in the mental trash bin and set it on fire. Because she was here now. On the last night of high school, she was here. And he was here for her.

"It's okay," he said, locking his eyes with hers. "You don't have to tell me. Whatever is going on, you don't have to say anything. I'm just really, *really* glad to see you. That's the only thing I want to say."

Gaia looked back into his eyes, and Ed saw something in her finally break. She fell forward and threw her arms around him, nestling her head on his shoulder, clasping her hands tightly behind his neck and squeezing for dear life. Ed grasped her waist tightly and shut his eyes. He could feel it in the quick contractions of her diaphragm. She had begun to cry silently on his shoulder, and it was making his heart break.

"I'm leaving, Ed," she said through her tears. "For good. And. . . I need to leave tonight, and I was on my way to the bus station, and I really didn't want to deal with anybody, but. . . I couldn't leave without saying goodbye to you. I couldn't do that."

Ed took a deep breath and tried not to punch himself in the face. He had always trusted his instincts. Always. Especially where Gaia was concerned. Even when Liz had talked about Florida, he'd known it didn't sound right. But *he* was the one who'd momentarily lost faith in their friendship. Not her. He was the one who'd stopped believing in their connection. And he would never make that mistake again. That is, if he even had the opportunity to make that mistake in the future. He still wasn't clear on the "future" part. . . .

"Gaia. . . I don't understand," he said. He lifted her head from his shoulder so he could get a better look at her. Tears had made her cheeks just as sopping wet as her hair. "Where are you going?"

Gaia stared at him in silence for far too long. This was clearly a question she didn't want to answer. Or maybe she didn't know the answer? "I'm leaving New York," she said. "It's time."

"But where?"

"Wherever."

Ed didn't even know what to say in response. Gaia was the only person he knew who could leave an entire life behind without even deciding where she was going first. He envied her in a way. But that didn't mean he could accept her terms.

"Are you sure?" he asked.

Gaia didn't even blink. "I'm sure."

The conviction in her tearstained eyes left Ed speechless. Speechless and hurting. He was losing her all over again. She had finally shown up just to disappear for good.

"Well, I'll come with you," he announced. And he meant it. There wasn't an ounce of wishful thinking there. He was just stating fact. If Gaia could up and leave the city, then so could he. He could go anywhere with her. Anywhere she wanted to go.

"No. You can't," she said. That was it. Just those three words spoken with such certainty—such absolute finality. It chopped Ed right off at the knees. It left his heart stumbling around again, trying desperately to regain its footing.

"Please don't worry, Ed," she said. "I'll be okay."

"Gaia. . . ," he said dubiously, "I just—"

"Ed, *please*," she begged. "You *don't* need to worry.

You know I can take care of myself. You're the one person on this planet who has always respected that. Please don't change now. Not now. *Please.*"

Ed looked in her eyes. He could see how important this was to her. He could see that the stakes were so much higher for her than they had ever been before. And more than that... he could see that even one wrong word could cut her so deep. This wasn't the Gaia he was used to: the girl with walls around her so high and so thick that it would take the end of a cold war to tear them down. Something had happened to her since the last time he saw her. Something big and bad enough to make those walls crumble. He had never seen her so raw and exposed. And he wasn't about to do *anything* to cut further into those open wounds. He just couldn't do that. Whatever she needed right now, that's what he had to give her. Just looking at her was killing him as it was.

"Okay." He nodded. "Okay..."

"Ed... Just say goodbye to me." She swiped the falling tears from one cheek with her forearm, and Ed automatically wiped the other cheek with his thumb. "Please. Say goodbye and promise me that we're both going to be okay."

He felt another one of the seams in his heart tearing open. All he had wanted for the past three hours was this—just a chance for one last proper goodbye. But the reality of it was so much worse than anything he could have conjured up in his head. Saying goodbye to her face. . . her actual face. . . that was a whole other level of pain. He didn't know if he could say goodbye. He still wasn't sure he could do it, despite how much it was clearly what she needed him to do.

But that was really the point. It wasn't just what she wanted him to do, it was what she *needed* him to do. And Ed would always place her needs above his own. That would be true for the rest of his life, no matter what happened.

He grabbed hold of both her hands, and he pulled her closer. There were a hundred million things he wanted to say. He wanted to beg her to stay. He wanted to take her back to his apartment and let her sleep for as long as she needed and stay as long as she needed and have bagels and coffee every morning for the entire summer. He wanted to get down on one knee and propose an immediate shotgun wedding in Vegas, and if she said yes, then he would pick her up in his arms and carry her out of that alley and all the way home if she asked. What he wanted most was just to be with her. To be with her for as long as they could possibly be together until the absolute end—whatever form that would take. He just wanted her to *stay.*

But if Gaia Moore said she was leaving, then she

was leaving. And neither Ed nor a fully armed SWAT team could possibly stop her. He'd already lived through the horrific experience of her leaving without saying goodbye. He wasn't about to live through it twice.

"Okay," he said. He forced himself to take deep breaths so as not to lose it. "Okay. . . Goodbye."

"Say the rest." She sniffled, squeezing his hands.

Ed swallowed hard. He suddenly realized that what he was swallowing were his tears. "Right," he uttered. He took another deep breath. "I. . . promise you that we are both going to be okay. . . particularly you," he added, feeling the need to be slightly more honest. "Me, I'm still working on it a little."

"No, you have to promise," she insisted. "You have to promise that you're going to be okay. I can't leave until you promise."

She was making it far too easy. All he had to do was not promise and she would stay.

"Gaia, can't you—?"

"No, Ed, if you make this any harder, then I will fall completely apart right now. *Please.* Don't make me regret coming here to say goodbye. I needed this. I needed to see you."

Ed took one last look at her fragile expression, and he convinced himself. She had left him with no choice but to spit out the words. He forced himself to believe it before he said it. "I promise that I am going to be okay," he stated. He bit down hard on his tongue. He was swallowing everything now—words, tears, blood, even. He swallowed it all down for her sake and he tried to appear as stable as he could. But just beneath the surface. . . just behind the face he knew she needed to see. . . he could feel himself unraveling.

"Okay," she said. "Okay. . . so. . . goodbye." She wiped her face again and tried to smile.

He wanted to wrap her up in his jacket and never let go. He wanted to hoist her over his shoulder and stash her away somewhere until she realized what a big mistake she was making—until she realized how much she needed him. But he did none of the above. All he could do was tighten every muscle in his face and say it. "Goodbye."

Gaia pulled her hands slowly out of his, and she turned toward the street.

But she turned around and she wrapped her arms tightly around the back of his neck. He wrapped his arms firmly around her waist as her lips fell against his. Her wet hair brushed against his face as she kissed him. He breathed in every ounce of her warm breath, and she pressed her body against his with more and more force. They needed this—for the same reasons or different reasons, it didn't even matter. They had made it through every imaginable disaster together. And they needed to share this one last kiss.

They finally let go, and Ed looked down at her, holding her face in his hands. "Gaia, just stay with me. Stay with me for the summer, and then you can leave."

"Ed." Her eyes were suddenly filled with regret, but they didn't move from his. Not for a moment. "I swear, if I could go back in time to us, to our night together and the next day, the day I should have *stayed,* I would do that. I would do that so fast. That was the happiest I've ever been. That was the closest I ever got. We were. . . I mean, you and me. . ."

"I know," he said. "You and me. Let's go back now. Let's go back to that day. We can start right now."

But Gaia's eyes only grew sadder and more resigned. "We can't. Our lives are changing now. Everything has to change. It has to. Understand?"

Ed shook his head slowly, but then he began to nod in spite of himself. Because he did understand. Beyond all the sadness, beyond everything his heart wanted so badly at this moment, there was a certain understanding of what she meant. Moving on. Growing older. Letting go of things you're convinced you absolutely need the most. For Ed that thing was Gaia. She was the thing he needed the most. And if he had any intentions of starting any kind of real life after high school. . . he apparently needed to let go of her. "I've been trying to," he admitted. "I've been working on it."

She smiled. "I love you," she said. "I know you know that."

"Oh, yeah, I know that." He smiled. His nonchalance was deeply ironic, and it made Gaia laugh. Which was all he had ever wanted to do.

"Okay," she said. She finally pulled away and backed a few steps down the alley. "Okay. . ."

"Okay. . . ," Ed croaked. "Please don't make me say goodbye again. I can't do it twice."

"I won't," she said. "We've said it."

"Right."

"Right, so. . . Right." She jumped back and gave him one last long kiss, and then she turned around and ran down the alley into the light of the street. She ran hard and fast, and she never looked back. Ed watched the last of her blond hair disappear around the corner, and he knew she was gone. For real this time. Gone.

But he had to admit. . . his vision for this night had come true. Maybe not exactly the way he'd imagined it. Okay, not at all the way he'd imagined it. But with Gaia, nothing ever was.

Ed was still going to go home and lie down in his tux and experience a hollow feeling of deep misery for an endless succession of days and nights.

But the fact remained. . . there was, indeed, such a thing as a soul mate. And Ed had the inexplicable feeling that he would have his for many years to come.

A Simple Plan

GAIA CLIMBED UP THE STEPS OF A Greyhound bus with nothing but the sopping wet clothes on her back. She gazed down the length of the bus's narrow aisle and began the slow search for a seat. She knew she looked like absolute hell. She looked just as burnt out and worn away as she felt. She watched as the passengers in each row flashed her dirty looks and whispered various asides to each other about the tragic state of America's youth. She passed row after row of seats until finally her eyes met with those of a serene old woman who did not pass judgment on her but rather offered her a most unexpected welcoming smile. It took all she had not to start crying again right then and there.

She plopped down next to the woman, in a state of pure exhaustion the likes of which she had never experienced without passing out. And finally. . . she could stop running.

It had only been a few blocks from that alley on Forty-seventh Street to Port Authority, but it had felt almost as long as the run from Skyler's as she tried to recover from saying goodbye to Ed.

She sat there squirming in her seat as she searched for some kind of emotional stability. Thoughts of Jake were still pounding on the door, as were thoughts of

Mary and now Ed. All those painful pieces of the past that she was trying to leave behind. It wouldn't be easy at first. She knew that. Moving on physically was a very different thing from moving on emotionally. There weren't just miles of ground to cover; there were miles of unresolved feelings, too, and Gaia had no idea how long it would take to heal or even if she ever *would* heal. She only knew that this was the first step: the bus's ignition and the shutting hydraulic door.

But as the engine began to rev up, Gaia was amazed to find that the physical movement actually did seem to have some kind of emotional effect on her. She found her entire body flooded with the most unexpected sense of relief the moment the bus rolled out from the tunnels of Port Authority to the late-night streetlights of New York. She watched the Walt-Disney-fied stretch of Forty-second Street disappear behind her, and it was almost like she could feel the city saying goodbye. Or not so much saying goodbye as just. . . letting her go. The city was such a living, breathing entity. It seemed to have a mind of its own. And in a strange way, even the city seemed to know the truth:

She was leaving it for good. She was never going to come back.

But the true relief didn't come until they'd turned onto the West Side Highway. When they hit the highway, Gaia finally found herself leaning back into her chair with a kind of relaxation that she had probably not experienced in the past five years. As the bright New York skyline faded out of view in her window, she actually let out a long exhalation. She was, in fact, so at ease for that moment that she didn't even mind when her serene elderly seatmate struck up a conversation.

"Where you headed?" the woman asked. She had a slight southern accent that Gaia couldn't quite place. Her eyes were kind, and so was her voice. She reminded Gaia a little of an older French actress she'd seen in a movie once, although Gaia couldn't remember the movie.

"Well. . ." Gaia laughed uncomfortably now that it was actually time to answer the question. "I'm going out to Ohio to visit my brother, D. I haven't seen him in a long time. He's staying with a friend of mine. But after that. . . to be honest. . . I don't even know."

"Ah, you're a voyager, huh?" The woman smiled.

"Um. . . I am now," Gaia said. A voyager. . . She actually liked the sound of that. It sounded epic somehow. Filled with majestic possibilities.

The old woman examined Gaia's profile for a bit longer, clearly waiting for her to say more. But Gaia didn't know what else to say. She was literally taking her life one minute at a time now.

"Well, where do you want to go?" the woman finally asked.

Gaia looked at her, and then she glanced away,

peering out at the dark Hudson River for an answer. The way the woman had asked, it seemed like such a simple question. *Where do you want to go?* A girl on a bus ought to know where she was going, right? But to Gaia, that question was everything but simple. It was, in fact, loaded with a very daunting sense of mystery.

She simply hadn't thought as far as where she actually wanted to end up. Once she had paid D a nice long visit, she had no sense of a final destination. She only knew where she *didn't* want to be anymore. She only knew what she had to leave. And that part of the mission was accomplished.

So, after looking fruitlessly to the river and the dark night sky for an answer, she ended up giving the woman the only honest answer she could think of.

"I don't know," she said. "Someplace where I can feel safe. Someplace where I can be happy. But I don't know where."

The old woman cocked her head and laughed. "Oh, that's an easy one," she said. Gaia could tell that she had somehow just tapped into a well of this woman's worldly wisdom. And she was glad. At this point she would take wisdom wherever she could get it.

"Let me tell you," the woman said, "I've been where you are. I was a bit of a voyager myself back in the day, and I've done the math on this one. All you've got to do is ask yourself: Where was the last place you felt truly safe and truly happy? And once you figure that out. . . you just go there." She threw up her arms as if to say, *Piece of cake!* "So? Where was it?"

It was a hell of a question. Truly safe? And truly happy? Gaia Moore? Nuh-uh. Three things not commonly used in the same sentence. When had she ever felt truly safe and happy without compromise? Without wondering when it was all going to explode in her face or someone else's? Without wondering when the inevitable facts of her life would set in and it would all fall apart in the most tragic way possible? No, she would have to go way back for that feeling. Way back.

But then, of course, she realized. That was where the answer was. It *was* way back. Way back in another time and another place, when she was basically another person. The key to her future was in her past. . . .

She turned to the woman as the sudden epiphany began to fill her with hope. *Truly safe and truly happy. . .*

"A house in the mountains," Gaia said, letting her eyes drift out the window as the night raced by. An involuntary smile crept up at the corners of her mouth. "When I was twelve years old. California. That's the last time I felt truly safe and happy. In California. My mother was there. And my father. We were all there. . . together." Gaia didn't feel the need to go into any more detail than that. She had enough problems with emotional stability as it was.

261

"California." The woman smiled. She nodded with approval. "Well, there you are. . . . Now you know where you're going."

Gaia looked into the old woman's eyes. Once again she had somehow made it all seem so very simple. And when Gaia really thought about it. . . she supposed it was.

Dear Dad,

*   Someone once said that you can't judge a man (or a woman) until you've walked in his (or her) shoes. And I suppose they're right. As I sit here writing this (sorry if the handwriting's a little shaky), I think I'm just beginning to get a sense of what it might feel like to walk in your shoes for a little while. And I think maybe that might not be such a bad thing in the long run (yes, I believe there may in fact be a "long run").*

*   I remember that night in Paris when you showed me all those letters you had written to me and never sent over the years—the ones that explained why you had to go away and how much you missed me. The ones that tried to explain why sometimes going away is really the safest and wisest choice for all parties involved. . .*

*   Well, I just wanted you to know, Dad, for the record, I think I'm starting to understand that concept—at least in theory. And most importantly. . .*

I forgive you. I do. From the bottom of my heart. I wish I could have understood it better when I was younger and not wasted so many years being angry at you—years I can't get back and emotional damage I probably can't totally repair—but still, I wanted you to know. I forgive you for all the times you've gone away. I know it didn't mean that you didn't love me or want what's best for me.

I want you to understand that I love you so much, and I will write you again very soon and tell you where I've ended up. But for right now. . .

It's my turn to go away.

And I know you understand. Because you've been in my shoes. So please don't worry. I think you know now that I can take care of myself.

I love you,

Gaia

Losers with no imagination
tend to get a little confused
about what it means to be an
"existentialist." I think for the
most part, when someone says
they're an existentialist, people
just assume that means they're
really depressed, they wear a lot
of black, and they read a lot of
Sartre or Camus.

   Well, I suppose that would
have been a pretty apt descrip-
tion of me, actually. But
that's just my point. Even *I*, a
self-proclaimed existentialist,
lost sight of the true meaning
of the philosophy. I think I
became one of those losers with
no imagination.

   The fact is, as far back as I
can remember, there's always been
someone else pulling the strings
in my life. No matter what I do,
I've always been falling into
someone's trap, part of someone
else's "grand design": Loki,
Ella, George, Natasha, Tatiana,
Yuri, Skyler, even that psychotic

son of a bitch Chris, who actually called himself "God." Talk about "grand design." I hope he rots in prison for the rest of his life.

But the point is, I've always believed that all those demented bastards were in charge of my fate. And I kept letting it happen again and again. I kept giving up all my power to them. I kept letting *them* make all the decisions about what god-awful tragedy was going to befall me next. And as long as I *truly* believed that my fate was already decided for me—that the tragedies were somehow inevitable—they just kept *happening*. Over and over. Until my own existence felt practically nonexistent.

But Loki has gone away. And the Rodkes have been taken in. There's nothing standing in my way now. No one left to pull my strings but me.

My predetermined life is over now. I am never again giving anyone the power to decide my fate

besides *me*. *I* decide. I make my
own fate. That is what it truly
means to be an existentialist.

And I have made my first truly
existential decision. I am
putting my past behind me. I am
leaving this city and I am
redesigning my life from scratch.

I will grieve. I will grieve
for all the people I've lost—all
the other victims of the puppet
show. I will grieve for Jake
every hour on the hour for a long
time to come. And I will miss Ed
like crazy every day. I'm not
forgetting my past. I'm just not
going to live in it anymore. From
this day forward, I will only
live in my future. The new future
that I am creating for myself.

It's so strange, really.
Strange that existentialism
always seems to be equated with
depression and despair. People
have it all wrong.

To be on your own. . . to make
your own fate—to be completely in
charge of who you are and what
you become. . . I think that is

the most hopeful thing in the world. That is a new feeling that I am just beginning to learn about: hope.

So I'm looking to the future now. My future in California. It's entirely unknown. And that's *beautiful*. I have finally graduated from my old puppet past. No more strings, no more restraints ever again. My fate is mine and mine alone.

I am, to put it simply, free.

a
look
back...

Yuri
(father to Katia and Natasha)

Oliver Moore   Thomas Moore—Katia Moore   Natasha Petrova
(brother to Thomas Moore)   (sister to Katia Moore)

"D" Moore   Gaia Moore   Tatiana Petrova
(brother of Gaia)   (daughter to Natasha Petrova)

When GAIA MOORE was young, she rescued her childhood friend from a pit bull's attack. A few years later she busted a thug who was beating on her babysitter. Soon enough her parents realized— their daughter was not like other girls. Multiple tests and studies revealed what Thomas and Katia had long suspected: Gaia simply couldn't feel fear.

As a CIA agent, TOM MOORE knew well enough the everyday dangers his daughter could potentially face—and of course, some of the less expected dangers that were, sadly, altogether too common in his life. As a result, he decided to train his daughter to defend herself. Gaia was a quick study, and she proved as capable an academic as she was an athlete. Tom, Katia, and Gaia moved to a cottage in the Catskills, where they existed almost completely in a world of their own.

Soon enough, though, Tom's twin brother, OLIVER, resurfaced. Oliver had also been trained as a CIA agent but had never achieved the recognition or prestige that his brother had, and he was deeply in love with his brother's wife. So there were some issues, needless to say. On a quest for revenge, Oliver gunned Katia down in her own kitchen, effectively ending Gaia's childhood.

Eventually Tom was called back to active duty. He placed Gaia in the care of a onetime colleague, GEORGE NIVEN, and his wife, ELLA. Tom rushed off on one mission after another while Gaia relocated to Perry Street, enrolling in the Village School. So while other girls worried about what to wear on the first day of school or what hairstyle was "in" that season, Gaia—ever her father's daughter and more aware of imminent threat than ever—was on the constant alert for danger.

Survival tactics. Ambush techniques. Methods of surveillance. And calculus.

Whoever said high school was easy?

Here's a peek at some highlights of Gaia Moore's senior year. . . .

ON GAIA

GAIA ON GAIA

"My name is Gaia. Guy. Uh. Yes, it's a weird name. No, I don't feel like explaining it right now. I'm seventeen. The good thing about seventeen is that you're not sixteen. Sixteen goes with the word *sweet,* and I am so far from that. You see, I have this handicap. Uh, that's the wrong word. I'm hormonally challenged. I'm never afraid. I just don't have the gene or whatever it is that makes you scared."

ED ON GAIA

"Do you get into fights *everywhere* you go?"

HEATHER ON GAIA

"Who the hell do you think you are?"

TOM ON GAIA

"In the case of a mugger or a purse snatcher going up against Gaia, I would frankly fear more for the criminal than for her."

SAM ON GAIA

"When I'm with her—when I even think of her—I feel things. I feel a wave brewing just out of reach, building and swelling into a breaker of dangerous proportions. Maybe that's what love is."

LOKI ON GAIA

"I take on all duties myself. Because I have no choice. And because Gaia deserves it. She deserves better than these thugs and lackeys I've thrown at her—she's so laughably superior to those drones. She deserves a captor with a genius equal to her own. She deserves me. And I her."

GAIA ON GAIA (AGAIN)

Some things I like:
Chess
Slurpees
Road Runner cartoons
Eye boogers
W. B. Yeats
Ed

Some things I don't like:
Four-dollar coffee drinks
Foster parents
Skim milk
Butterflies
Baking soda toothpaste
Myself

A thing I hate:
Being away from my dad

FROM THE FILES OF OLIVER "LOKI" MOORE

Subject: Gaia Moore

Age: 17

Character traits: Confrontational, socially maladjusted. Self-conscious. Street smart. Book smart. **Fearless.**

Physical abilities: Karate, jujitsu, *muay thai,* mountain climbing, boxing, wrestling, speed, strength, agility, accuracy.
*Note: *Any period of increased or excessive exertion is typically followed by a "blackout" period where the subject is rendered physically drained and, in most cases, unconscious for at least a brief period.*

Mental abilities: Multilingual (at least 4 languages, possibly more), code-breaking, computer-hacking, advanced mathematics, and analytical reading skills.

Action: Complete surveillance of subject at all times. I want info.
*Note: *Subject is not to be harmed under any circumstances.*

SLOPPY FIRSTS
(from the back of Tammy Deegan's notebook)

Ed's first love: Heather

Ed's first sexual encounter: Heather

Heather's first college boyfriend: Sam

Sam's first love: Gaia

Gaia's first love: Sam

Gaia's first kiss: Sam

Gaia's first boyfriend: Sam

Gaia's first sexual encounter: Ed

FROM THE FILES OF OLIVER "LOKI" MOORE

Subject's Addresses

Perry Street: Subject resided in brownstone with ex-CIA agent George Niven and his wife, Ella. George developed a professional friendship with Tom Moore during their days in the Agency but ultimately turned and collaborated with Loki. Ella was a collaborator from the early days.

Reasons for move: Ella was killed by an assassin who mistook her for Gaia. George was later killed by his collaborators when he proved no longer useful to Loki.

Mercer Street: Two-bedroom apartment subject shared with Tom Moore in an effort at "family stability."

Reasons for move: Tom was called away on Agency business; subject temporarily moved to the **Moss** family apartment (**see Appendix A, *Mary Moss***).

Upper East Side: Subject was brought to this residence with Tom Moore and his then-partner (work and romantic), Natasha Petrova. Tom Moore and subject resided at this location with Ms. Petrova and her daughter, Tatiana.

Reasons for move: Natasha was revealed to be the sister of Katia Moore, working in conjunction with Organization head Yuri; Tom Moore was once again called away on Agency business.

Note: Natasha and Tatiana have since been apprehended and incarcerated.

Bank Street: Subject's last known address; boardinghouse for children of Agency officials. Subject shared residence with two other minors, monitored by Agency-appointed housemother.

APPENDIX A

Subject's Known Friends

Ivy: Friend from before subject's move to New York City. NO FURTHER INFORMATION AVAILABLE.

Heather Gannis: Eighteen years old, romantic ties to Sam Moon (HIGHLY SUSPECTED THAT SUBJECT WAS DIRECT CAUSE OF THE BREAKUP) and Ed Fargo. Long dark hair, blue eyes. Extremely attractive by conventional standards. Was at top of social hierarchy until incident with beta-model fearless serum rendered her temporarily blind. Initial dislike of subject. Recently released from boarding school for blind students.

Mary Moss: Seventeen years old, loud, impulsive, combative. SUBSTANCE ABUSE ISSUES. Tall and v. thin, bright, curly red hair and green eyes. Striking, not pretty. Stable home environment.
*Note: *Terminated at the hands of an assassin posing as a drug dealer due to interference with our ultimate agenda.*

Liz Rodke: New social queen at Village School, daughter and heir apparent of Rodke Pharmaceuticals empire to be divided with two older brothers. Down-to-earth. Long blond hair (NOT TO BE CONFUSED WITH THAT OF

SUBJECT; USUALLY WORN DOWN RATHER THAN TIED BACK), bright smile.

*Note: *L's involvement in the most recent plot against the subject remains undetermined.*

FROM THE VILLAGE SCHOOL YEARBOOK

MELANIE YOUNG'S GUIDE TO
DOWNTOWN SHOPPING

Antique Boutique: *The* place for vintage styles—all in fabulous conditions and a funky setting.

Patricia Field: The official stylist of *Sex and the City*. Need I say more?

Broadway Shoes: A selection to rival even Heather Gannis's closet (Jk, Heather!! Lol!).

Fresh: Cosmetics and skin care. Your face will thank you. Your boyfriend probably will, too.

Mavi: They *will* carry your favorite jeans. The ones that make your butt rival Jennifer Aniston's. And no, I'm not kidding (would I joke about something like *that*?).

Tower Records: True, the downtown location is a little limited, but hey—it's within walking distance of school.

PEOPLE WHO HAVE TRIED TO KILL ME
(from Gaia Moore's laptop)

(This list does *not* include ancillary attackers,
i.e., skinheads in Washington Square Park, etc.)

1. Uncle Oliver. Ollie. Or Loki. Whatever name he's using, he's got a plan for me. He swears he'd never hurt me. Yeah, right.

2. David: Loki's protégé, another freak who couldn't feel fear. Seemed to have some crazed competitive thing with me. Also, posed as a potential date. Nice.

3. CJ: Still not sure what his problem was. Suspect he was working for Ella.

4. Ella: She actually put a hit out on me. But she sorta made up for it when she apologized to me, posed as me, and took the fall herself.

5. Skizz: Mary's drug dealer. Savory sort.

6. George: Uh, apparently not so much my father's "old friend from the Agency."

7. Natasha: Again, ticked off that her daughter was being passed over in favor of me.

Please—Tatiana can *have* all the glory of the "Organization." I just kind of want a permanent address.

8. Tatiana: See above.

9. The doctors at Fort Myers: Weren't so thrilled when I uncovered their operation and busted my long-lost brother out of there.

EAT HERE NOW: GAIA'S GUIDE TO
FINE DINING IN NYC
(from a scrawling on the back of
Gaia Moore's calculus test)

Benny's Burritos: Any upgrade in the kitschy, Southwestern decor would ruin the upbeat charm of this lively Mexican joint. A great value; monster burritos.

Dojo: No-frills vegetarian. The tattoo-and-body-piercing show is a bonus at no extra charge.

Falafel King: Fulfills at least 2 of your daily servings of "fried." Cheap, messy, and spicy. A perfect after-school—or instead-of-school—snack stop.

Gray's Papaya: This 24-hour stand has zero atmosphere, but where else can you get two dogs with all the trimmings—and something to drink, too!—for two bucks?

Krispy Kreme: More of a religion, actually, than a doughnut.

Murray's Bagels: Carbalicious bliss. Atkins, schmatkins. Get there early or stand in line.

Odessa: I like my grease with grease on the side. Good for late-night munchies or a morning-after breakfast.

Kind of a hole in the wall but with huge portions, low prices, and quirky waitresses with unintelligible accents—do you really care?

Starbucks: A gift from the gods above or a slow and painful path to hell? You make the call. (If you want to piss them off, order "coffee, black.")

Taylor's: Heaven in a pastry shell. Accept no substitutions! And take a free sample while you're there.

Veselka: Hearty Ukrainian fare at gentle prices! When you want to be reminded of your mother. Or when you want to be reminded of my mother.

THE HOOKUP
(from Tammie Deegan's journal)

Heather and Ed

Heather and Sam

Gaia and Sam

Heather and Ed

Gaia and Ed

Heather and Josh

Ed and Tatiana

Gaia and Jake

Ed and Kai

PEOPLE WHO HAVE BEEN KILLED
AS A RESULT OF HANGING AROUND WITH ME
(from Gaia Moore's laptop)

1. David: Not sure. Think Loki "disposed" of him based on his bad behavior.

2. Mary: Either killed by Skizz or killed by someone posing as Skizz. The fun is in the guessing (yes, that's sarcasm).

3. Ella: Met similar fate as Subject #1.

4. Mike Suarez: Sam's roommate who got played in one of Loki's twisted games.

5. Josh Kendall: Heather's "boyfriend" who turned out to be one of Loki's lackeys. The good news? Yeah, Loki cloned him. Wouldn't be surprised if there were a few more "Joshes" still running around.

6. Sam: Shot dead. But—ha ha!—not really dead. Just injured, captured, and held. Always a fun time when your true love comes back from the dead. Very *Dynasty*.

FROM THE FILES OF OLIVER "LOKI" MOORE
THE MANY FACES OF FEAR

SUBJECT: GAIA MOORE

Experience of fear: None. Gaia Moore is born without the fear gene. Incapable of experiencing fear.

Result: Gifted with extraordinary traits; i.e., reflexes, strength, speed.

Treatment: Special training so as to allow her to use her talents to her utmost advantage.

Experience of fear: Gaia takes our experimental serum in order to experience fear.

Result: Panic and mental instability.

Treatment: Given medical treatment to reverse the effects of the drug.

Experience of fear: Gaia allows herself to be a subject in an experimental gene therapy program intended to create the sensation fear, conducted by Rodke Pharmaceuticals.

Result: Hyper-reaction. Terror, inability to cope.

Treatment: None needed. Effects fade in time.

SUBJECT: HEATHER GANNIS

Experience of fear: Typical—fraught with adolescent insecurity. Allows herself to be test subject of experimental "fearless" serum created from DNA taken from Gaia Moore.

Result: Temporary fearlessness, ultimately giving way to foolhardy and daredevil behavior. Delusions of immortality. Ultimately rendered temporarily blind.

Treatment: Both fearlessness and blindness faded over time.

SUBJECT: OLIVER MOORE (SELF)

Experience of fear: Typical, though often displaced/suppressed by way of rigorous intelligence training. Manipulated through use of "fearless" serum to similar state as Ms. Gannis. "Subject" eventually lost consciousness, falling into a comatose state.

Treatment: Basic life-sustaining measures. Ultimately woke from coma independently. No permanent side effects have been noted.

APPENDIX B
"INVINCE"

A drug that acts much like the "fearless" serum, Invince can be ingested in tablet form. The subject experiences a profound high that begins with a basic lack of fear but usually develops into acute delusions of immortality and imperviousness. Presently widespread in downtown Manhattan, distributed by one supplier who refers to himself as "God" but who has, in fact, been identified as Christopher Rodke, of Rodke Pharmaceuticals. Prevalence of Invince in downtown neighborhoods has led to a vast increase in violent crimes and injuries.

FROM THE VILLAGE SCHOOL YEARBOOK
TAMMIE DEEGAN'S RAVES AND FAVES

Best place for a mocha-java fix: Starbucks. But be on the lookout for a certain hulking blond with a bad sense of spatial relations!

Best location for a blind school benefit: Pravda, of course!

Best place to work it out*: Crunch!
*(Best trendy workout: Pilates. Or cardio striptease, you fox!)

Best after-school activity (after Starbucks and shopping): Bowlmor Lanes.

Best movie house: Angelika, for the upscale café fare. But when are they gonna soundproof the walls?

Best reason to put on lip gloss in the morning: Jake Montone (sorry, J—couldn't resist!).

Best venue for an inexcusably swanky impromptu bash: The Mercer Hotel (thank you, Chris and Liz!).

Best reason to blow your diet: Monster chocolate-chip cookies at Grey Dog's Coffee.

Best cheesy date: A horse-drawn carriage in Central Park.

Best place for a "DTR*": Sushi Samba.
*("Define the relationship" conversation)

Best defense of the "natural look": Do the initials "GM" ring any bells?

ON LOCATION
GAIA MOORE'S PERSONAL TRAVEL JOURNAL

They say **Paris, France,** is the city of love, and "they" weren't messing around! When Dad and I headed off there to spend some QT together for the first time since I was twelve, we were really feeling the love! We had barely set foot in the country when we were being followed by men—probably Loki's—who wanted us dead. But as I always say, a day without a barroom brawl is like a day without sunshine. Nothing like an attack at a local wine bar to take the bloom off the proverbial rose. Good thing I know how to take care of myself. Forget Paris—big time.

Of course, if it's sun, rest, and relaxation you're looking for, you can't do better than **Fort Myers, Florida.** Oh, sure, there's the pesky issue of electroshock therapy to contend with, and—oh, yeah—you just might encounter a long-lost brother you never knew you had. And then somehow find yourself wearing dresses and makeup and grinning at everyone like some moronic girlie-girl. But all you need is one square peg (think Angelina in *Girl, Interrupted*) to remind you of who you really are, and before you know it, you'll be busting out. All hell and whatever. Thank God for boyfriends with savior complexes!

Speaking of which, if you're going to go to **Siberia** (which, frankly, I can't recommend) and you hope to rescue your CIA agent father who's been captured by the enemy, well, then—and this I can't stress enough—you simply must be sure to bring along his borderline insane rogue agent brother. Bonus points if said brother has tried to kill you more than once. But I digress. The point I was making was that really, nothing brings two people together like a stint riding the rails in a foreign country under constant threat of attack. So if your boyfriend offers to come with you, by all means—bring him along!

FROM THE VILLAGE SCHOOL YEARBOOK
SENIOR SUPERLATIVES FROM MEGAN STEIN

Most likely to succeed: Chris Rodke. Can you say "heir apparent"?

Most like to succeed without really trying: Ed "Shred" Fargo. I mean, the boy will try anything twice. Just an all-around solid citizen. And cute, too!

Most likely to make a fabulous comeback: Heather Gannis. I hear she's doing really well, and if anyone can turn things around, it's our girl.

Most likely to become a top supermodel: Tatiana Petrova. I mean, if anyone can find her.

Most likely to incite maximum heartbreakage: Jake Montone. 'Nuff said.

Most likely to have fun no matter what: Kai Katsura. Has anyone ever seen her in a bad mood?

Most likely to become stylist to the stars: Megan Stein.

Most likely to become the next Joan Rivers: Carrie Longman.

Most likely to become America's sweetheart: Liz Rodke. That toothpaste grin. Those tawny locks. That sunny disposition. The disposable cash. The road is paved, my sister.

Most likely to be arrested/recruited by the FBI: Gaia Moore.

SIBLING RIVALRY
(observed by Thomas Moore)

The Sibs: Oliver and myself, Thomas Moore
The Issue: I was the strong one from the time that we were small children. Oliver had a physical condition that made him weak, and later, in Agency training, it became clear that he didn't have my aptitude for code breaking and other paramilitary skills. Oliver met my beloved future wife Katia Petrova, but soon afterward she fell in love with me.
The Outcome: Oliver ultimately shot Katia and killed her. He claims her death was accidental. He sees Gaia as his own rightful child—all the more so because he and I, as identical twins, share DNA. He has spent most of his adult life as a rogue agent, trying to bring about my demise and looking for ways to lure Gaia to his side. Despite moments of true remorse and regret, he is not trustworthy.

The "Sibs": Gaia Moore and David Twain
The Issue: Though not technically Gaia's twin, David Twain was trained and manipulated by Loki. He developed strong competitive issues with Gaia, whom he saw as his sister. Once he came to the Village School, he posed as a would-be-suitor to catch her with her defenses down and destroy her.

The Outcome: Obviously Gaia escaped. Furious, Loki disposed of David before he could do any further damage.

The Sibs: Heather and Phoebe Gannis
The Issue: Both Gannis girls were beautiful and popular, but as the elder, Phoebe took the pressure to an extreme. Where her mother and sister were "health conscious," Phoebe developed an acute eating disorder, and the hospital fees she incurred while in treatment sent her family into debt.
The Outcome: Heather was ashamed that her family didn't have the kind of money that her friends' families had and would go to any lengths to hide that fact. For that reason, when Ed learned of an experimental treatment to help him walk again, she discouraged him from exploring the possibility (doing so would have rendered him ineligible for a sizable settlement). Heather and Ed broke up over this issue.

The Sibs: Ed and Victoria Fargo
The Issue: Victoria felt ashamed of Ed when he was wheelchair-bound after his skateboard accident. But she got over it quickly once he was walking—and dating a social queen like Heather Gannis—again.
The Outcome: Ed is not impressed by Victoria's fair-weather-sib attitude.

The Sibs: Gaia Moore and Tatiana Petrova

The Issue: Tatiana, actually Gaia's first cousin, was trained and groomed since day one to take over in the "Organization," a terrorist group run by Gaia's grandfather, Yuri, that operated without the knowledge of Gaia, Tom, or even Loki—until Natasha and Tatiana blew the lid off the gig. Ultimately Yuri decided that Tatiana wasn't a worthy heir and shifted his attentions toward getting Gaia under his auspices. Consumed with jealousy, Tatiana and her mother, Natasha, concocted an elaborate scheme to undo Gaia and her father.

The Outcome: Gaia and her father set up a sting operation to take Natasha and Tatiana down, resulting in the two of them being captured and imprisoned indefinitely.

The Sibs: Chris and Skyler Rodke

The Issue: The two boys are poised to take the mantle of Rodke Pharmaceuticals—but there can only be one right-hand man. Though Dr. Rodke fully intended to hand over a piece of the pie to each of his sons, Chris wasn't content with just a piece. He didn't want to be second runner-up and he resented his brother's status as firstborn and golden child.

The Outcome: Dr. Rodke and Skyler assigned Chris the task of distributing a beta model of their

"Invince" tablets to the lowlifes in Washington Square Park, figuring it was a more efficient means of testing the drug's efficacy than any controlled environment. But Chris had plans to take his power position and abuse it. Either way, it looks like a stalemate. . . .

CRUNCHING NUMBERS
(from a napkin found in Sam Moon's pocket)

Boyfriends Gaia has stolen from Heather Gannis: 2

Dresses Gaia owns: 2

Parties Gaia has attended since she came to the Village School: 5

Number of those parties that didn't end in social disaster: 1

Long-lost relatives that Gaia has discovered: 4

Times Gaia has confused her father with her uncle: 2

Times Loki has confused anyone else with Gaia: 1

Times Katia confused Loki with Thomas: 2

People Gaia knows who have returned from the dead: 3

Times Gaia has undergone severe alterations in personality: 3

Boys who've pretended to be interested in Gaia in order to carry out plots against her: 2

Secret hospitals or labs from which Gaia has escaped: 2

People who've been able to match Gaia at chess: 2

People whom the FOHs don't rag on: 0

Girlfriends Tom Moore has courted: 1

Girlfriends Tom Moore has courted who have tried to kill him: 1

Girlfriends of Tom Moore who have turned out to be his deceased wife's sister: 1

Agents and colleagues who have turned against Tom: 3

Times a friend or relative of Gaia's has been kidnapped, killed, or otherwise threatened: 9

Times Gaia and her father have attempted to have a "normal life": 3

Times Gaia attempted to forgive Loki for everything he'd done: 1

Times Loki betrayed that trust: 1

People Gaia trusts in the world: 1

An unusual year, to put it mildly . . .

They say whatever doesn't **KILL YOU** only makes you **STRONGER.** Which really tells you all you need to know about **GAIA MOORE** (who, it might be noted, was pretty freakin' strong to begin with). High school may be over, but **GAIA'S ADVENTURES ARE CLEARLY JUST BEGINNING. . . .**

Turn the Page for an exciting sneak peek at:

FEARLESS FBI

Every now and then, when I have absolutely exhausted every other possible option, I allow myself to look back on my teens. And I cringe with embarrassment. The word "lost" just wouldn't do those years justice. "Confused" wouldn't really cut it either. More extreme terms are required to describe me back then. "Cosmically depressed" maybe? "Tragically Misinformed" is more like it.

Of course, my teens only ended a year ago, but still, some of it seems so far away now—just a murky gray cloud in my head. Names and faces from the Village School in New York …Tammie Deegan and Megan Stein and the rest of the FOHs. I've already forgotten the details of their faces. With each year at Stanford they turned more and more into poorly drawn cartoons in my head; clichéd characters played by bad actresses in another mediocre movie about bitchy cliques and high school growing pains.

But other memories feel so
fresh in my head it's like my two
years of college never even happened. The look on Ed Fargo's
face when I turned around and
left him for good in that dark
alley on 47th Street. And of
course, Jake. Watching the life
fall from his eyes is not an
image I will forget any time
soon. In fact, it took until
about a month ago to finally stop
seeing those lifeless eyes in
every one of my dreams.

But the dreams did stop, and
time kept on passing. And now
that I finally have some real
distance from it all, I can allow
myself an occasional reflective
moment like this one, and I can
make at least one conclusion with
absolute assurance: When it comes
to my teenage years . . . I had
absolutely no clue.

Some of this madness I can
attribute to hormones. Some of it
I can attribute to the fact that

my teenage years did in fact
suck. I lost a lot of people I
loved. I sustained an infinite
number of cuts and bruises. I saw
way too much blood, and I stood
at death's door way too many
times. But in truth, I think the
real culprit here is a demon more
powerful than hormones, more powerful than an empirically crappy
life, more powerful than death
even—stronger than any evil mas-
termind or weapon of mass
destruction. It is a merciless
disease that can send any teenage
girl into a massive unrecoverable
tailspin. And I was no exception…

Low self-esteem. That is the
insidious disease. It makes
skinny girls starve themselves
and pretty girls chop up their
faces. It makes us forget who we
are, and it makes us want to be
something else. Anything else,
really. Anything with an *"er"*
attached to the end: Prett* er*,
smart*er*, rich*er*, or in my case
normal*er*. Okay, there's no such
word, but don't let that cloud

my point. My point is this: In
my personal opinion, low self-
esteem is the most rampantly
uncharted cause of death in the
world. It turns short unattrac-
tive men into tyrannical murder-
ous dictators. It's the primary
reason people get drunk off
their asses and drive too fast
in their cars. It makes lonely
alienated kids kill themselves
or go on mass murdering sprees.
It made a gifted, reasonably
attractive girl like me hate
myself with a deep passion, and
pretty much everyone else, too.
To put it quite simply, it made
my teenage life a rather dismal
experience and I doubt I'm alone
on that one. And I've been suf-
fering from the disease since
the age of twelve, and only now,
almost ten years later, am I
beginning to go into remission.

   Why am I finally recovering at
the ripe old age of 20? Because I
met someone. And I *don't* mean a
boy. That is the biggest myth of
them all; that a boyfriend can

cancel out years of low self-
esteem with a gorgeous smile and
professions of love. That is a
big fat ugly illusion, and the
sooner my gender figures that one
out, the sooner we'll all be on
the road to recovery. No, I
didn't meet a boy, I met a woman
named Jennifer Bishop. Special
Agent Jennifer Bishop.

She walked into the Stanford
University gym while I was pummeling a punching bag with roundhouse kicks, and she asked me
point blank if I'd ever considered a life in law enforcement.
I, of course, told her no. Why
would I possibly want a life in
law-enforcement after everything
I'd been through—after everything
my father had been through? This
was at the end of my two year
stint at Stanford. This was three
months ago, before the summer,
when I still wasn't sure I wanted
a life in anything.

But Agent Bishop was almost as
stubborn as I am. And just as
blunt, too. She said some things

to me that no one has ever said,
or at least, she put them in a
way that no one has ever put
them. And for at least one moment
in that conversation, I admit
that I could actually see it. I
could see the pall of self-pitying narcissism lift from my life
for a split-second. I could see
how much time I'd pissed away on
self-imposed alienation. And I
could see these four words that
suddenly made an enormous amount
of sense. Four words that felt
like they could actually be a
glimpse of my future:

Special Agent Gaia Moore.

Francine Pascal's
FEARLESS
FBI

Sharper. Older.
More dangerous than ever.

A new series from Simon Pulse

As many as 1 in 3 Americans
who have HIV... don't know it.

TAKE CONTROL.
KNOW YOUR STATUS.
GET TESTED.

To learn more about HIV testing,
or get a free guide to HIV and
other sexually transmitted diseases:

www.knowhivaids.org
1-866-344-KNOW